7406 1390

# TIMEPOCALYPSE #3

ABDO
Spotlight

DARK HORSE COMICS

PopCap

Written by **PAUL TOBIN**
Art by **RON CHAN**
Colors by **MATTHEW J. RAINWATER**
Letters by **STEVE DUTRO**
Cover by **RON CHAN**

President and Publisher **MIKE RICHARDSON**
Editor **PHILIP R. SIMON**
Assistant Editor **ROXY POLK**
Designer **KAT LARSON**
Digital Production **CHRISTINA McKENZIE**

Special thanks to **LEIGH BEACH, SHANA DOERR, A.J. RATHBUN, BRENNAN TOWNLEY, JEREMY VANHOOZER,** and everyone at PopCap Games.

DarkHorse.com | PopCap.com

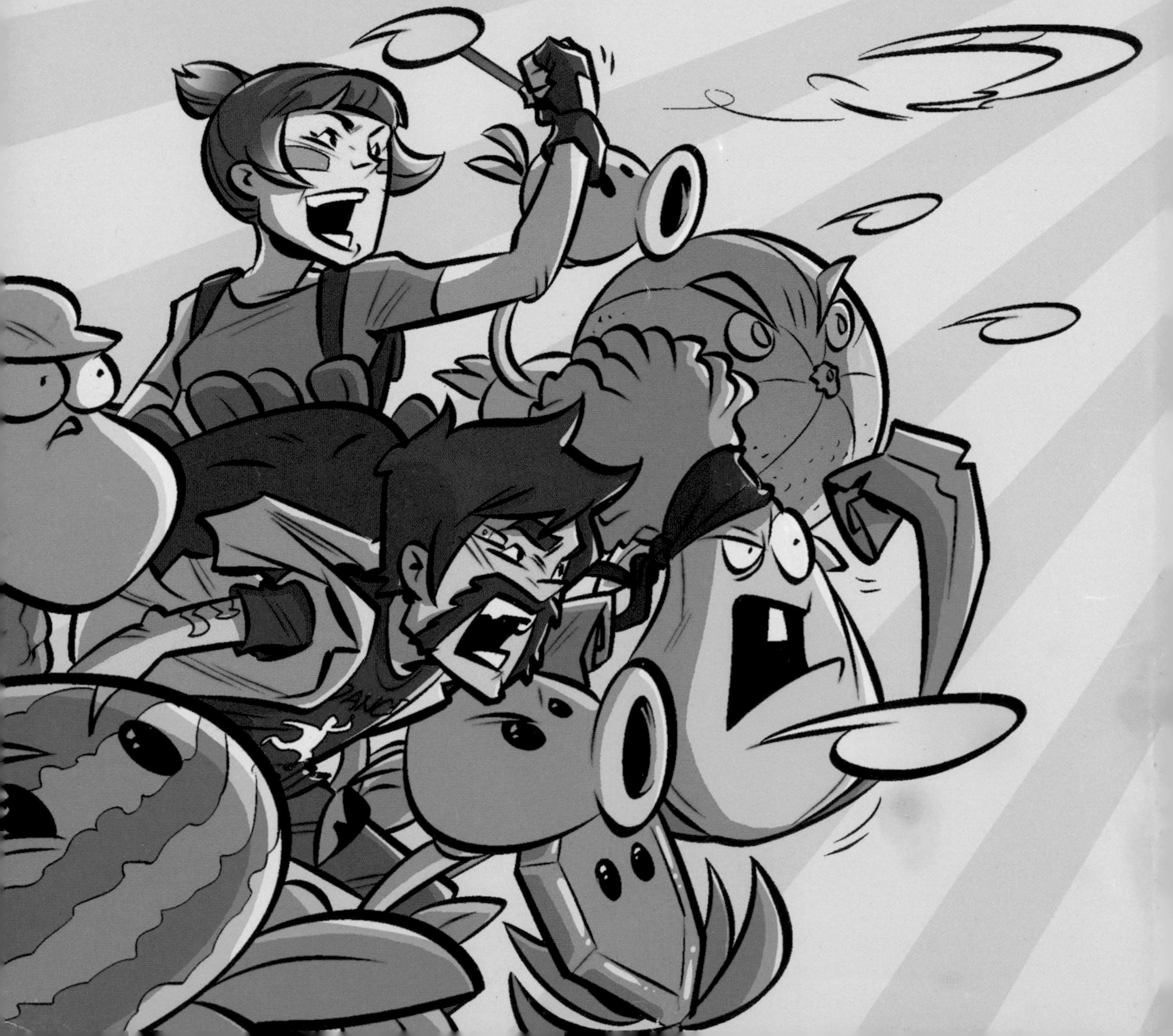

# PLANTS VS. ZOMBIES™

## TIMEPOCALYPSE #3

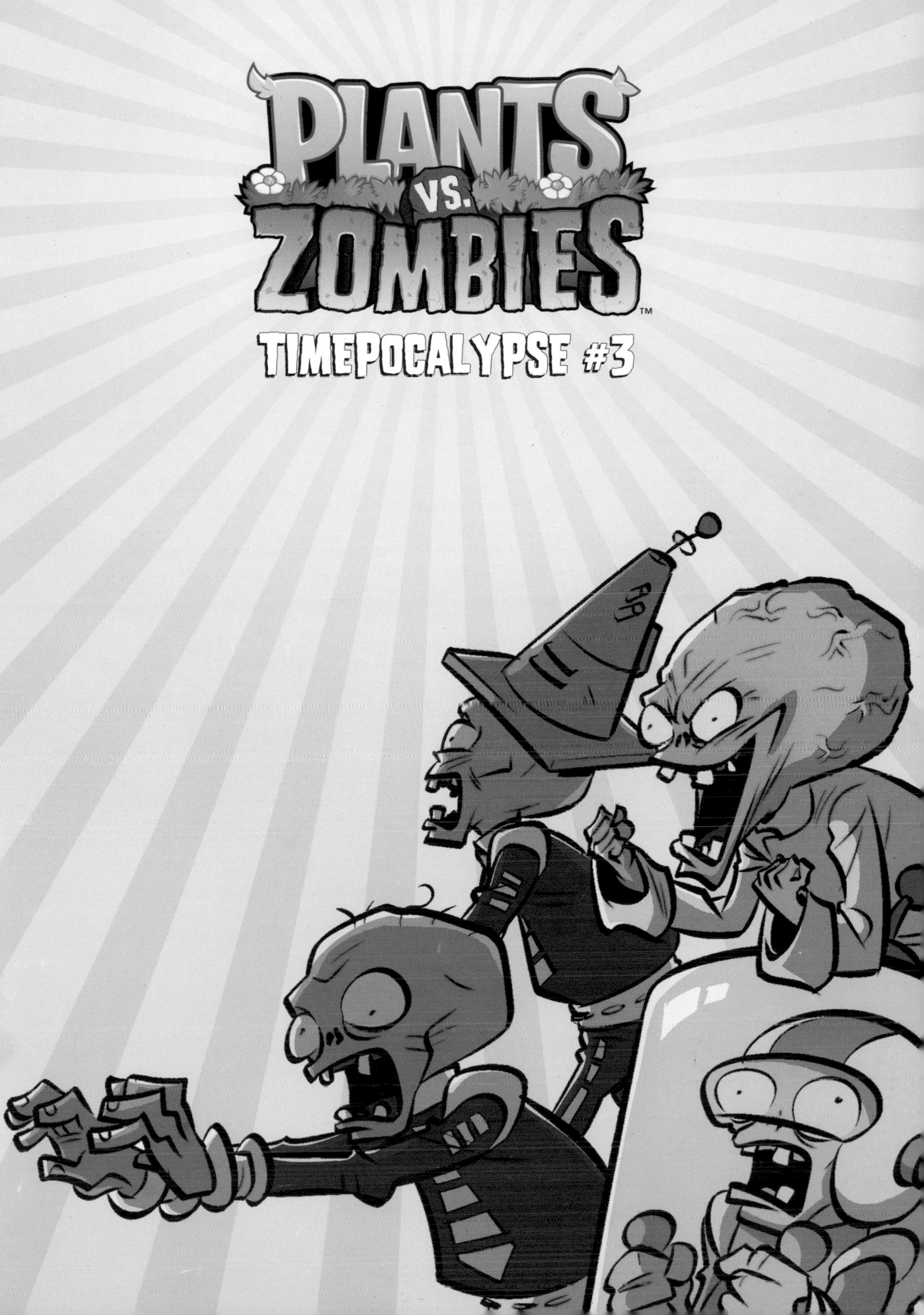

**ABDOPUBLISHING.COM**

Reinforced library bound edition published in 2017 by Spotlight, a division of ABDO, PO Box 398166, Minneapolis, Minnesota 55439. Spotlight produces high-quality reinforced library bound editions for schools and libraries.
Published by agreement with Dark Horse Comics.

Printed in the United States of America, North Mankato, Minnesota.
042016
092016

THIS BOOK CONTAINS
RECYCLED MATERIALS

Originally issued as Plants vs. Zombies: Timepocalypse #5 and Timepocalypse #6 by Dark Horse Comics in 2014.

## PUBLISHER'S CATALOGING IN PUBLICATION DATA

Names: Tobin, Paul, author. | Chan, Ron ; Rainwater, Matthew J., illustrators.
Title: Timepocalypse / by Paul Tobin ; illustrated by Ron Chan and Matthew J. Rainwater.
Description: Minneapolis, MN : Spotlight, [2017] | Series: Plants vs. zombies
Summary: When Zomboss's sun vacuum is blown up and scattered throughout time and space, Nate and Patrice race against the zombies to see who can gather all the missing pieces first.
Identifiers: LCCN 2016934738 | ISBN 9781614795438 (v.1 : lib. bdg.) | ISBN 9781614795445 (v.2 : lib. bdg.) | ISBN 9781614795452 (v.3 : lib. bdg.)
Subjects: LCSH: Time travel--Juvenile fiction. | Plants--Juvenile fiction. | Zombies--Juvenile fiction. | Adventure and adventurers--Juvenile fiction. | Comic books, strips, etc.--Juvenile fiction. | Graphic novels--Juvenile fiction.
Classification: DDC 741.5--dc23
LC record available at http://lccn.loc.gov/2016934738

**Spotlight**

A Division of ABDO
abdopublishing.com

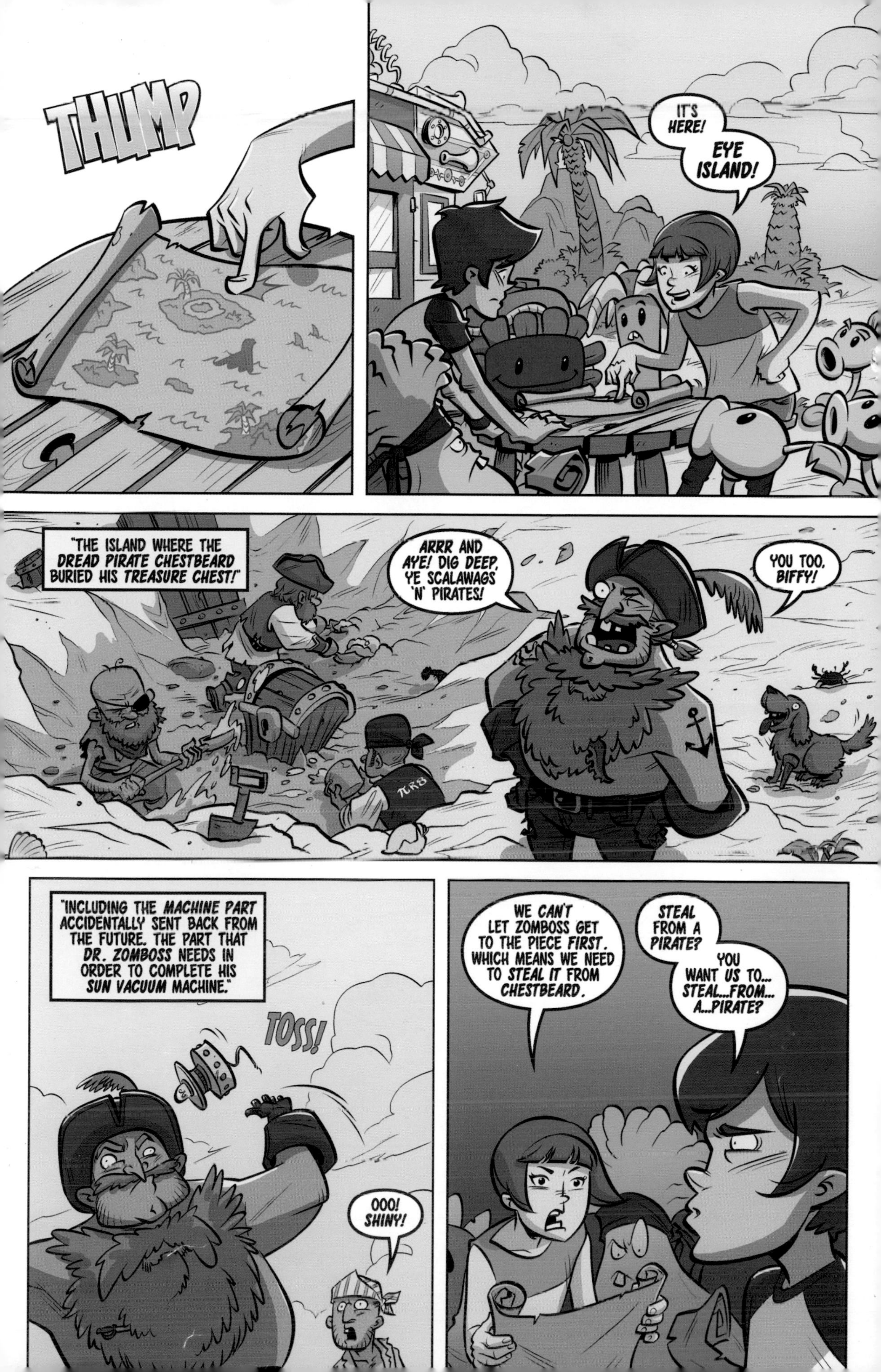
THUMP
IT'S HERE!
EYE ISLAND!
"THE ISLAND WHERE THE DREAD PIRATE CHESTBEARD BURIED HIS TREASURE CHEST!"
ARRR AND AYE! DIG DEEP, YE SCALAWAGS 'N' PIRATES!
YOU TOO, BIFFY!
"INCLUDING THE MACHINE PART ACCIDENTALLY SENT BACK FROM THE FUTURE. THE PART THAT DR. ZOMBOSS NEEDS IN ORDER TO COMPLETE HIS SUN VACUUM MACHINE."
TOSS!
OOO! SHINY!
WE CAN'T LET ZOMBOSS GET TO THE PIECE FIRST. WHICH MEANS WE NEED TO STEAL IT FROM CHESTBEARD.
STEAL FROM A PIRATE?
YOU WANT US TO... STEAL...FROM... A...PIRATE?

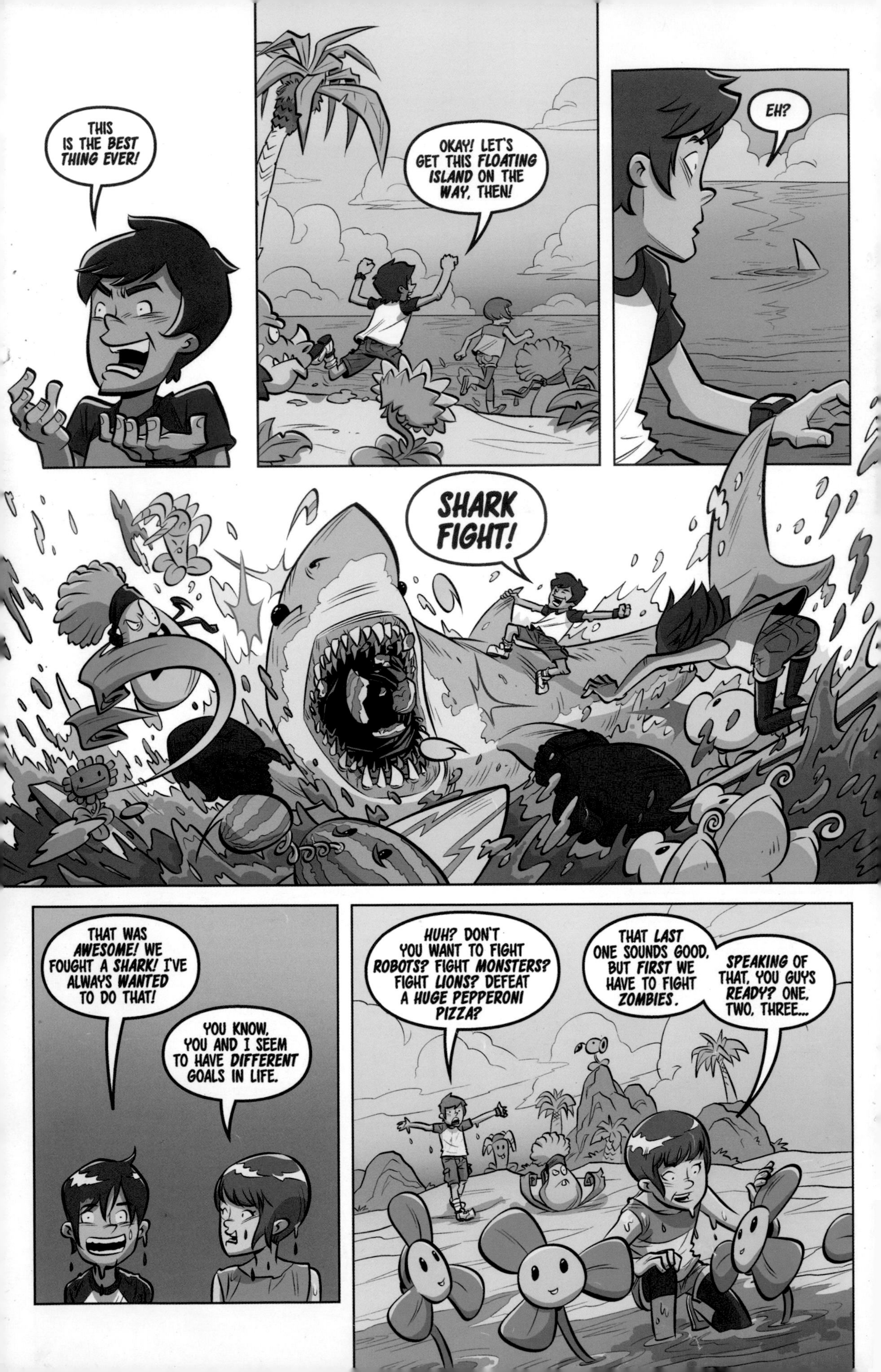
THIS IS THE BEST THING EVER!
OKAY! LET'S GET THIS FLOATING ISLAND ON THE WAY, THEN!
EH?
SHARK FIGHT!
THAT WAS AWESOME! WE FOUGHT A SHARK! I'VE ALWAYS WANTED TO DO THAT!
YOU KNOW, YOU AND I SEEM TO HAVE DIFFERENT GOALS IN LIFE.
HUH? DON'T YOU WANT TO FIGHT ROBOTS? FIGHT MONSTERS? FIGHT LIONS? DEFEAT A HUGE PEPPERONI PIZZA?
THAT LAST ONE SOUNDS GOOD, BUT FIRST WE HAVE TO FIGHT ZOMBIES.
SPEAKING OF THAT, YOU GUYS READY? ONE, TWO, THREE...

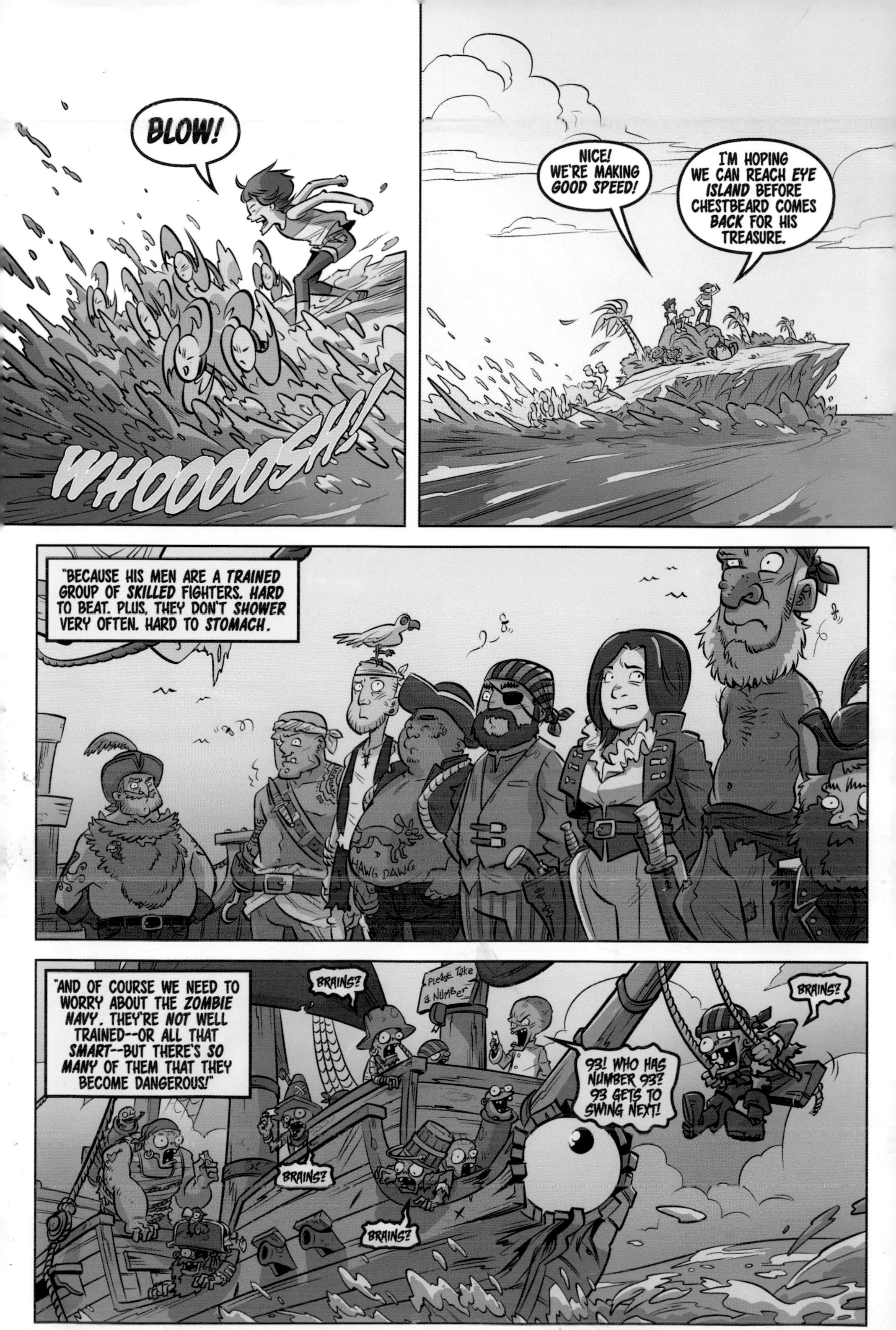
BLOW!
WHOOOOOSH!
NICE! WE'RE MAKING GOOD SPEED!
I'M HOPING WE CAN REACH EYE ISLAND BEFORE CHESTBEARD COMES BACK FOR HIS TREASURE.
"BECAUSE HIS MEN ARE A TRAINED GROUP OF SKILLED FIGHTERS. HARD TO BEAT. PLUS, THEY DON'T SHOWER VERY OFTEN. HARD TO STOMACH.
HAWG DAWG
"AND OF COURSE WE NEED TO WORRY ABOUT THE ZOMBIE NAVY. THEY'RE NOT WELL TRAINED--OR ALL THAT SMART--BUT THERE'S SO MANY OF THEM THAT THEY BECOME DANGEROUS!"
BRAINS?
Please Take a Number
BRAINS?
93! WHO HAS NUMBER 93? 93 GETS TO SWING NEXT!
BRAINS?
BRAINS?

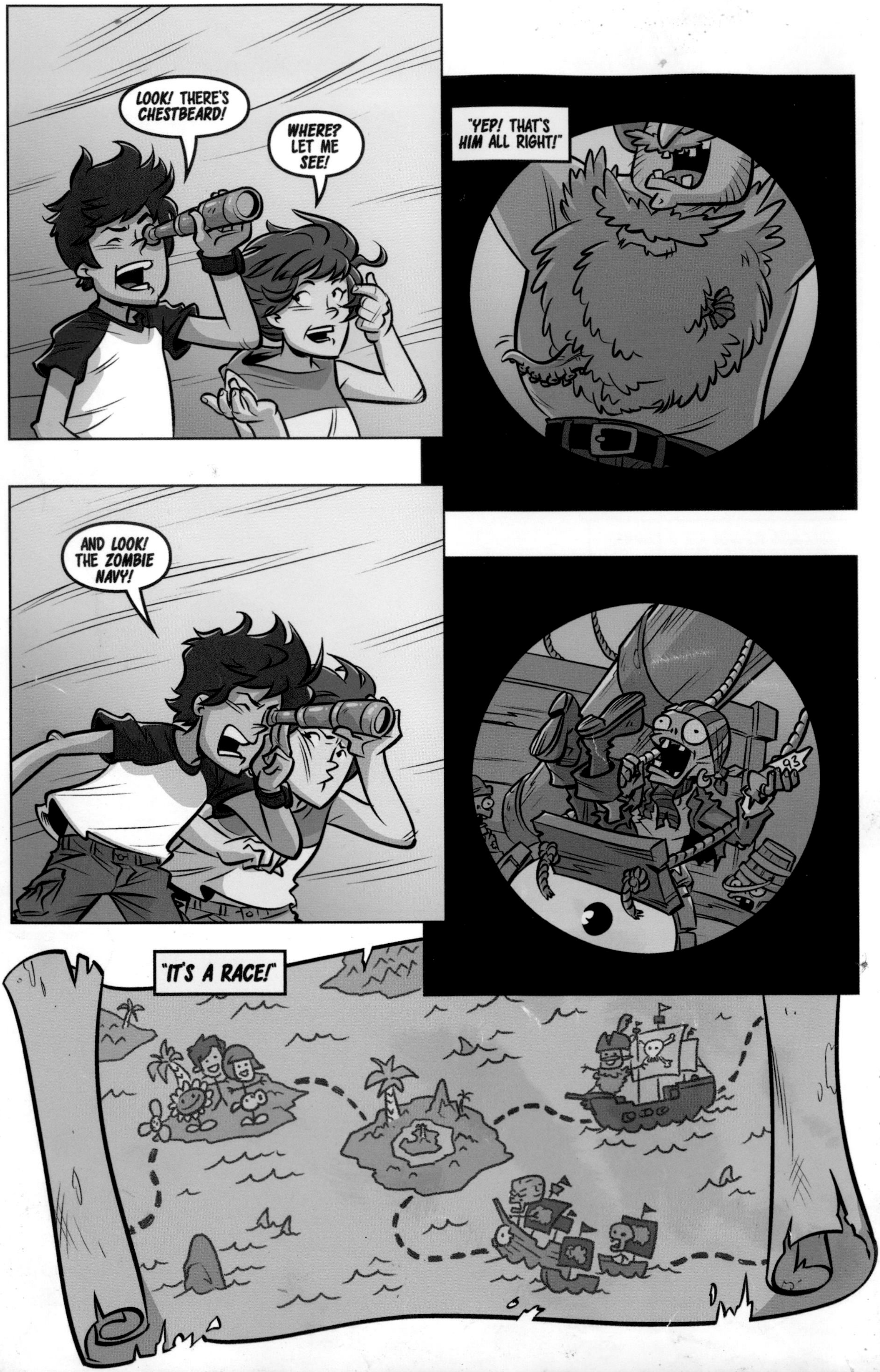
LOOK! THERE'S CHESTBEARD!
WHERE? LET ME SEE!
"YEP! THAT'S HIM ALL RIGHT!"
AND LOOK! THE ZOMBIE NAVY!
93
"IT'S A RACE!"

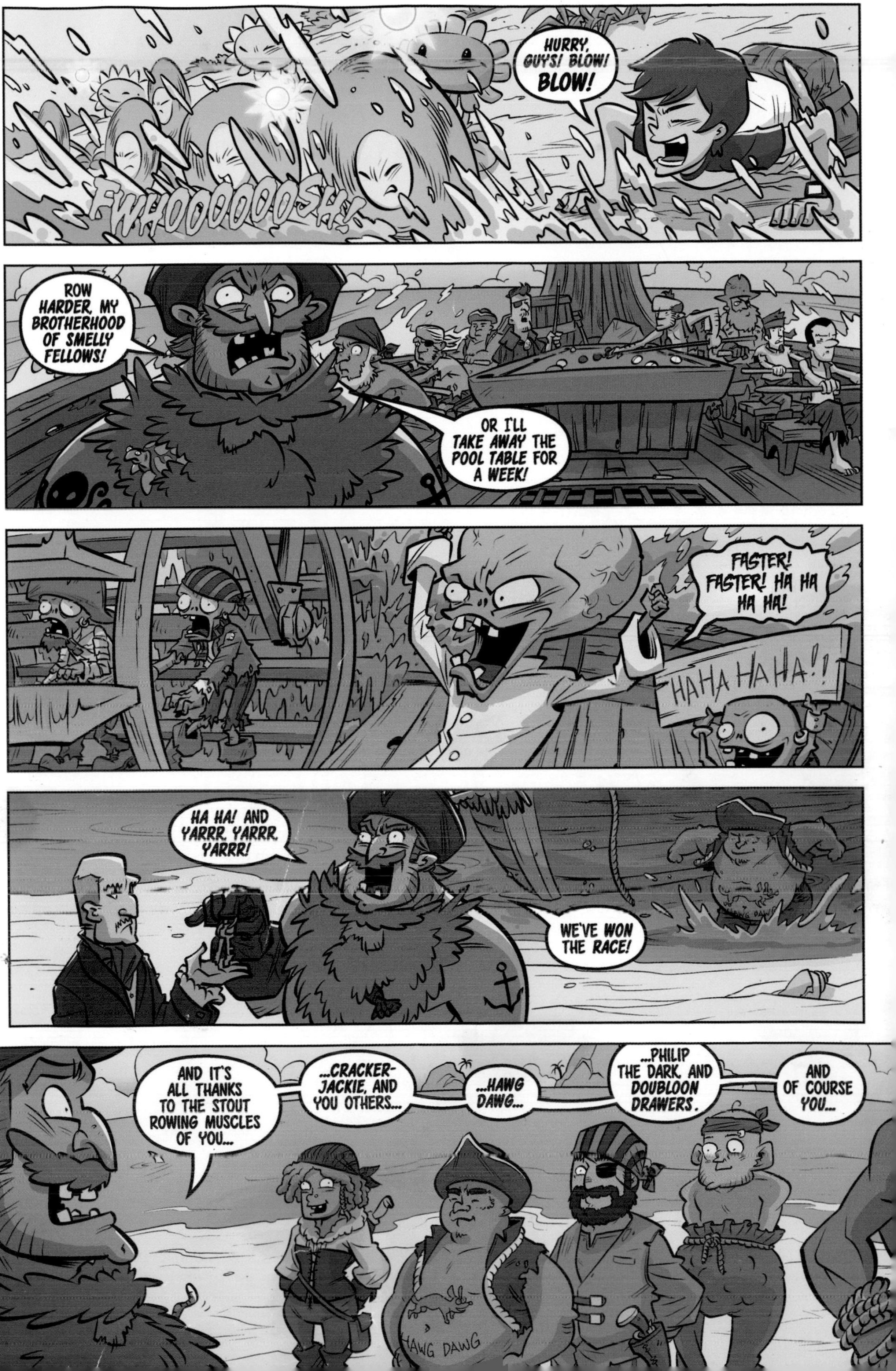
HURRY, GUYS! BLOW! BLOW!
FWHOOOOOOOSH!
ROW HARDER, MY BROTHERHOOD OF SMELLY FELLOWS!
OR I'LL TAKE AWAY THE POOL TABLE FOR A WEEK!
FASTER! FASTER! HA HA HA HA!
HAHA HAHA!!
HA HA! AND YARRR, YARRR, YARRR!
WE'VE WON THE RACE!
AND IT'S ALL THANKS TO THE STOUT ROWING MUSCLES OF YOU...
...CRACKER-JACKIE, AND YOU OTHERS...
...HAWG DAWG...
...PHILIP THE DARK, AND DOUBLOON DRAWERS.
AND OF COURSE YOU...
HAWG DAWG

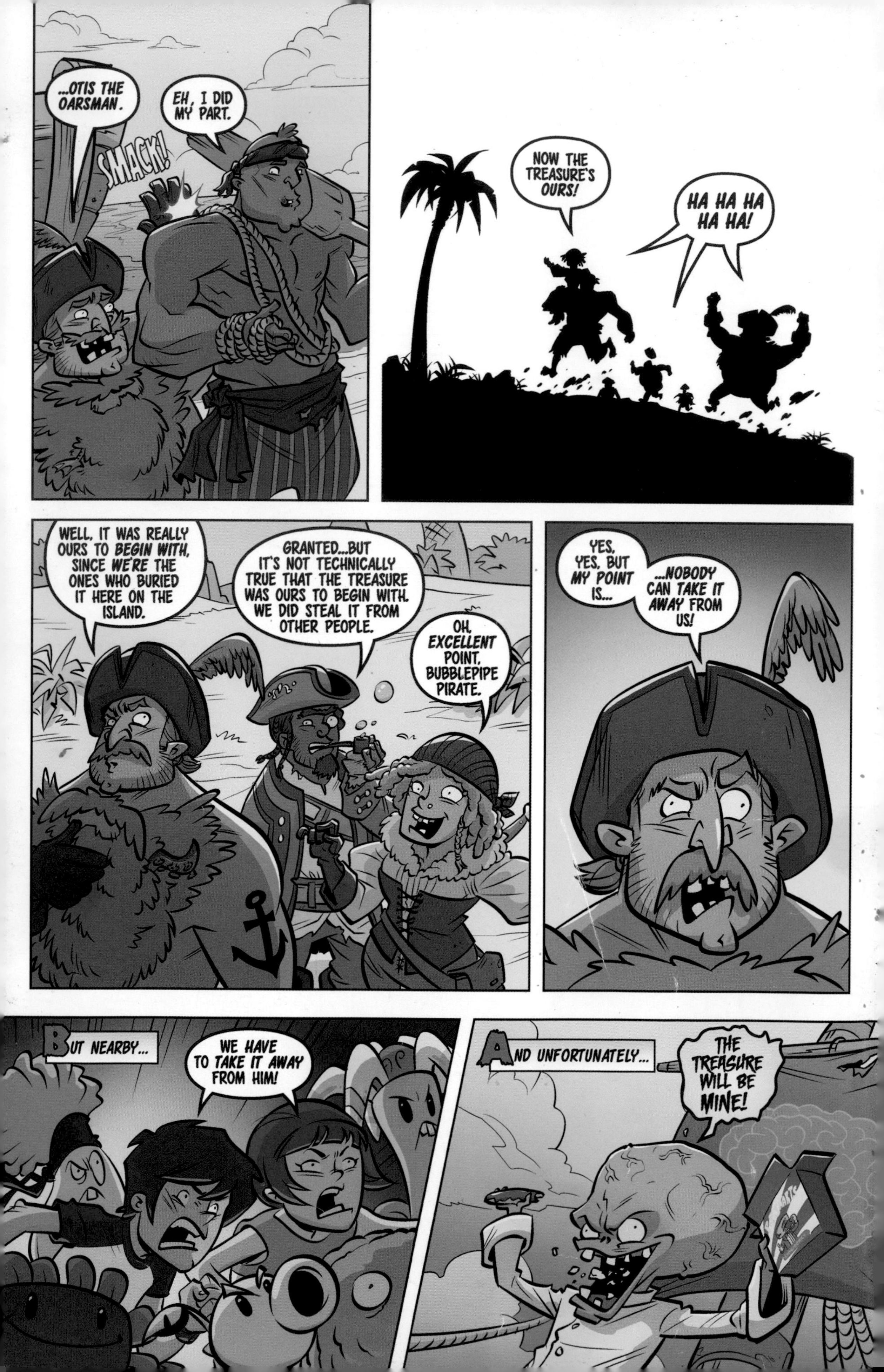
...OTIS THE OARSMAN.
EH, I DID MY PART.
SMACK!
NOW THE TREASURE'S OURS!
HA HA HA HA HA!
WELL, IT WAS REALLY OURS TO BEGIN WITH, SINCE WE'RE THE ONES WHO BURIED IT HERE ON THE ISLAND.
GRANTED...BUT IT'S NOT TECHNICALLY TRUE THAT THE TREASURE WAS OURS TO BEGIN WITH. WE DID STEAL IT FROM OTHER PEOPLE.
OH, EXCELLENT POINT, BUBBLEPIPE PIRATE.
YES, YES, BUT MY POINT IS...
...NOBODY CAN TAKE IT AWAY FROM US!
BUT NEARBY...
WE HAVE TO TAKE IT AWAY FROM HIM!
AND UNFORTUNATELY...
THE TREASURE WILL BE MINE!

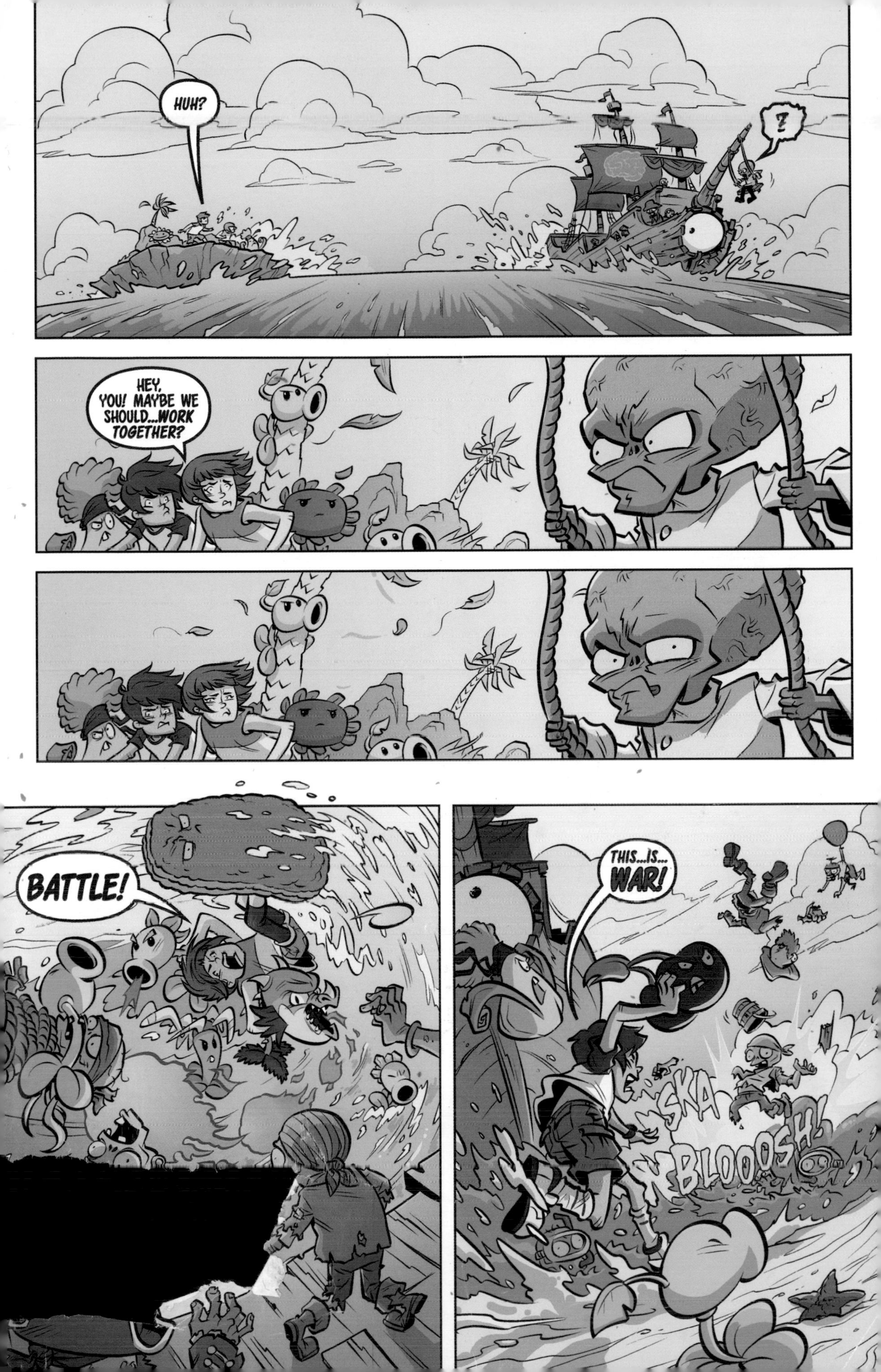
HUH?
?
HEY, YOU! MAYBE WE SHOULD...WORK TOGETHER?
BATTLE!
THIS...IS... WAR!
SKA
BLOOOSH!

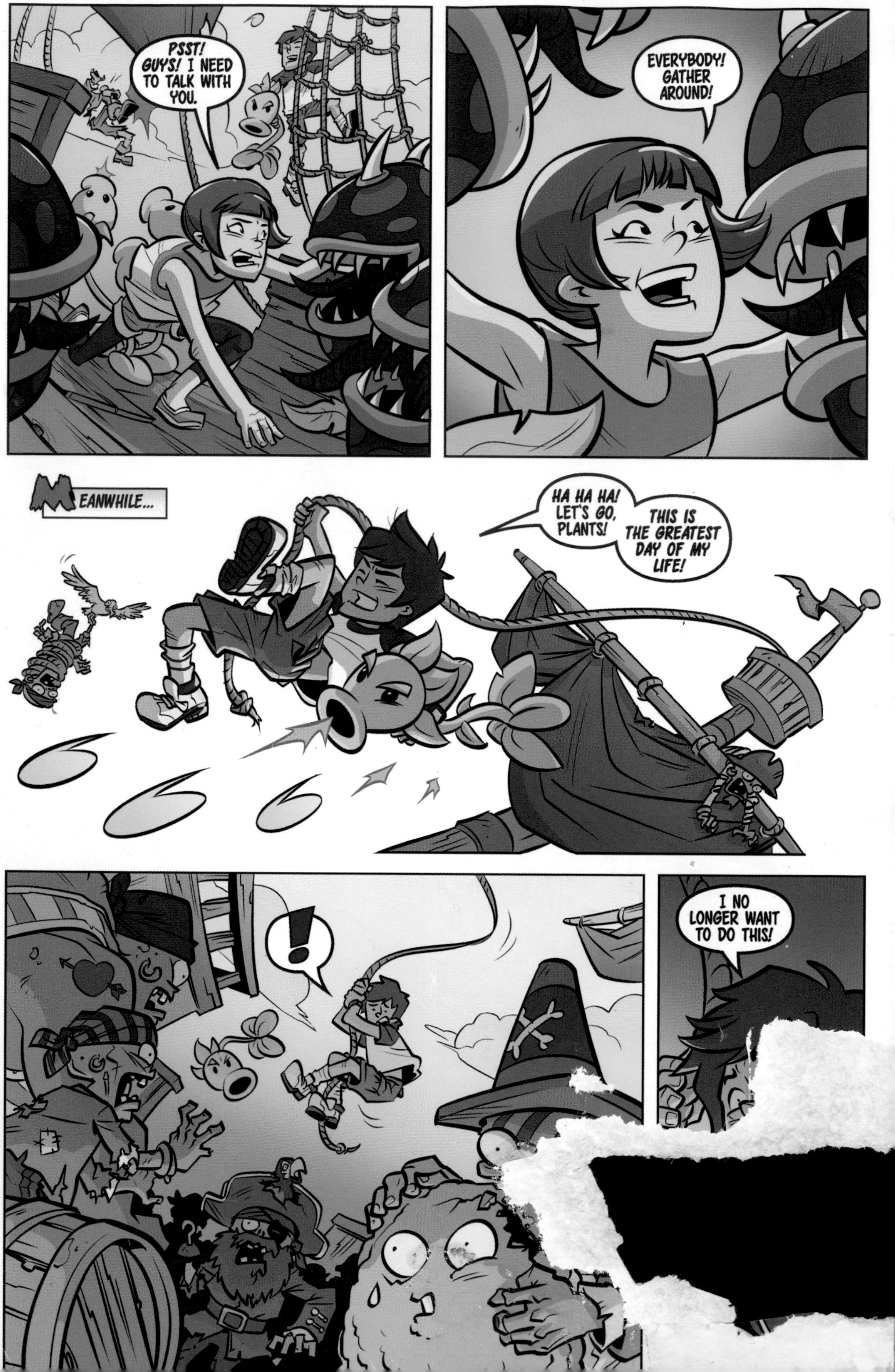
PSST! GUYS! I NEED TO TALK WITH YOU.
EVERYBODY! GATHER AROUND!
MEANWHILE...
HA HA HA! LET'S GO, PLANTS!
THIS IS THE GREATEST DAY OF MY LIFE!
!
I NO LONGER WANT TO DO THIS!

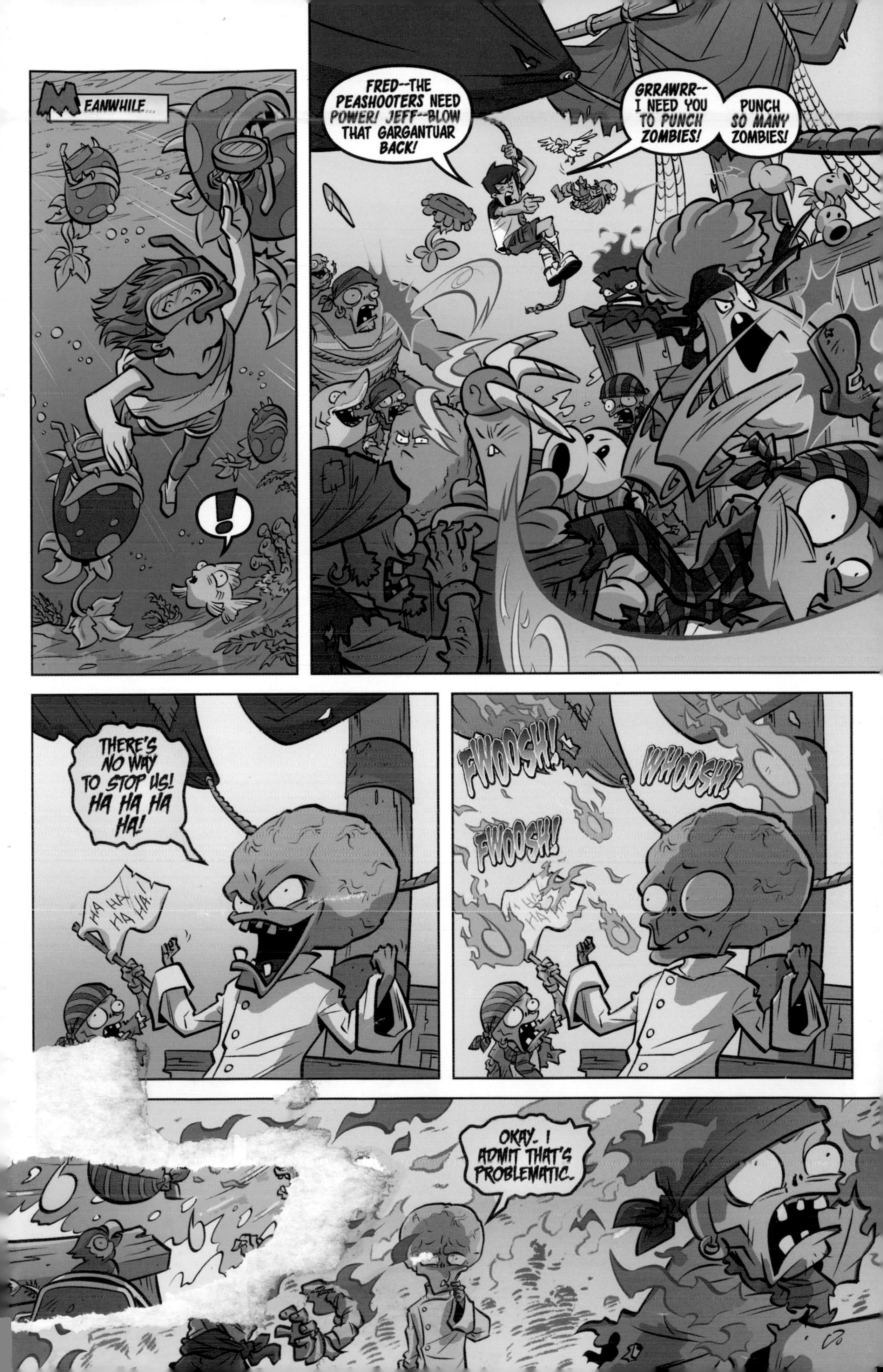
MEANWHILE...
!
FRED--THE PEASHOOTERS NEED POWER! JEFF--BLOW THAT GARGANTUAR BACK!
GRRAWRR-- I NEED YOU TO PUNCH ZOMBIES!
PUNCH SO MANY ZOMBIES!
THERE'S NO WAY TO STOP US! HA HA HA HA!
HA HA HA HA!
FWOOSH!
WHOOSH!
FWOOSH!
OKAY. I ADMIT THAT'S PROBLEMATIC.

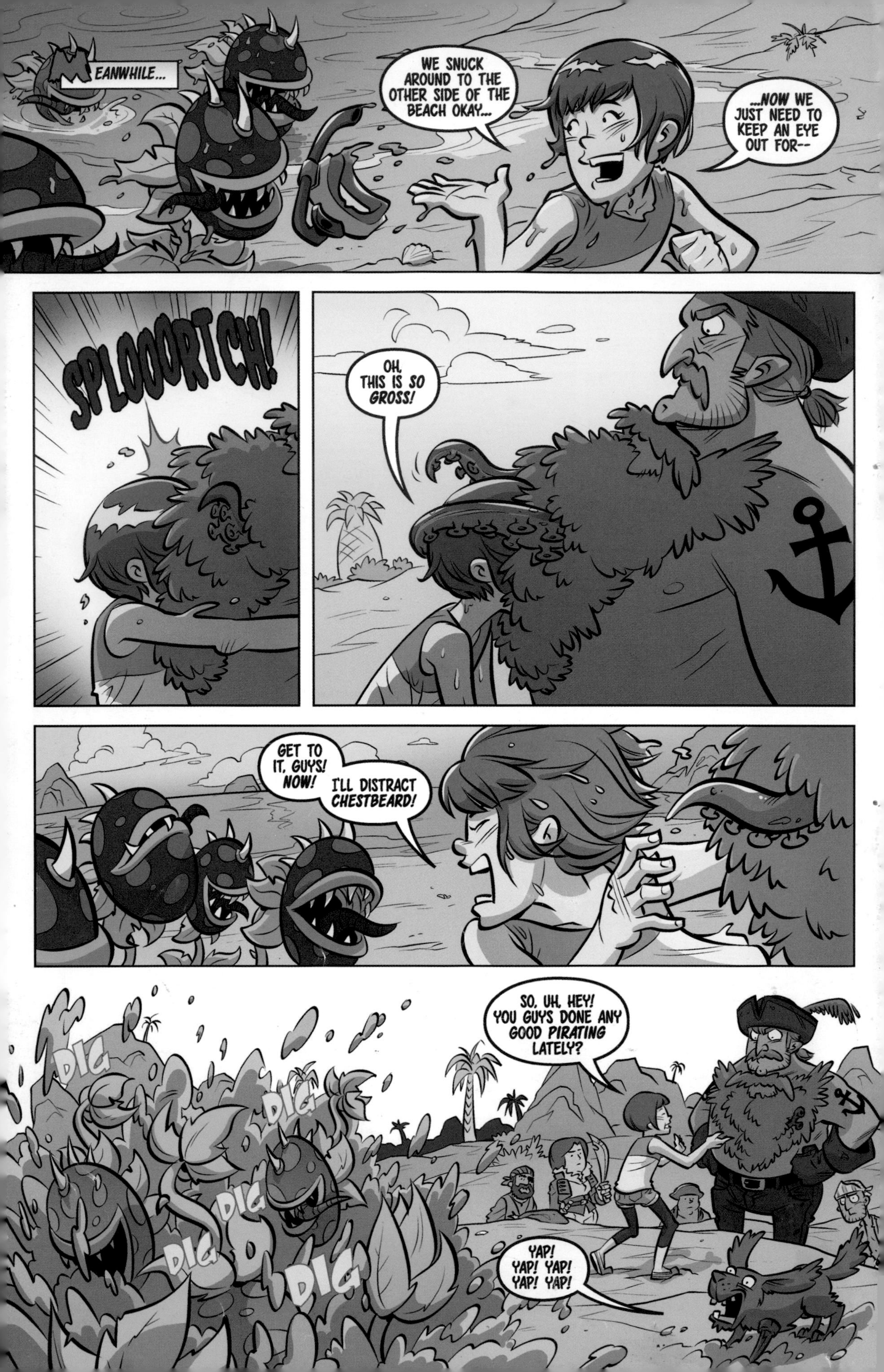
MEANWHILE...
WE SNUCK AROUND TO THE OTHER SIDE OF THE BEACH OKAY...
...NOW WE JUST NEED TO KEEP AN EYE OUT FOR--
SPLOOORTCH!
OH, THIS IS SO GROSS!
GET TO IT, GUYS! NOW!
I'LL DISTRACT CHESTBEARD!
SO, UH, HEY! YOU GUYS DONE ANY GOOD PIRATING LATELY?
DIG
DIG
DIG
DIG
DIG
YAP! YAP! YAP! YAP! YAP!

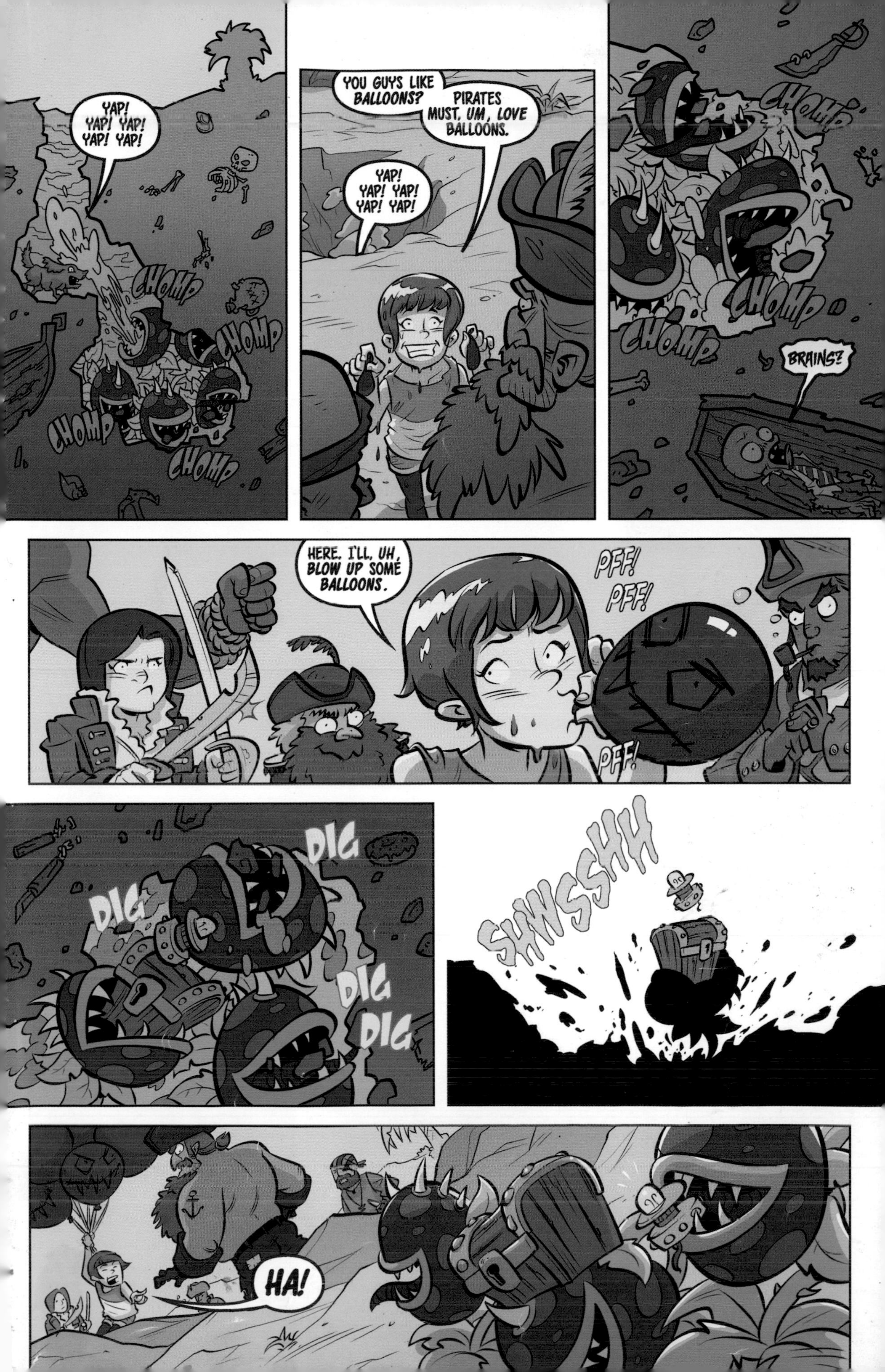
YAP! YAP! YAP! YAP! YAP!
CHOMP
CHOMP
CHOMP
CHOMP
YOU GUYS LIKE BALLOONS?
PIRATES MUST, UM, LOVE BALLOONS.
YAP! YAP! YAP! YAP! YAP!
CHOMP
CHOMP
CHOMP
BRAINS?
HERE. I'LL, UH, BLOW UP SOME BALLOONS.
PFF!
PFF!
PFF!
DIG
DIG
DIG
DIG
SHWSSHH
HA!

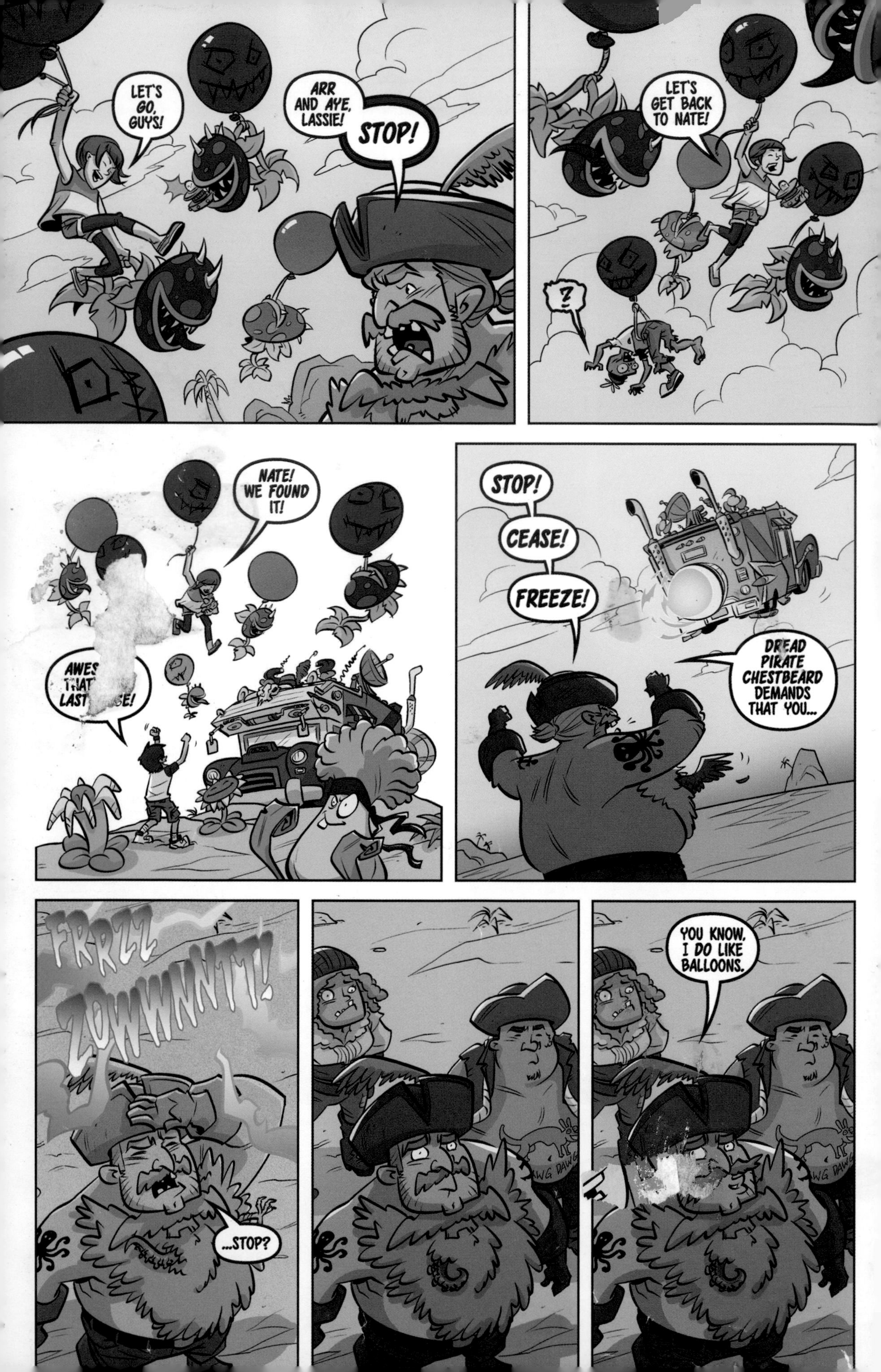
LET'S GO, GUYS!
ARR AND AYE, LASSIE!
STOP!
LET'S GET BACK TO NATE!
?
NATE! WE FOUND IT!
STOP!
CEASE!
FREEZE!
DREAD PIRATE CHESTBEARD DEMANDS THAT YOU...
FRRZZ ZOWWNNTT!
...STOP?
YOU KNOW, I DO LIKE BALLOONS.

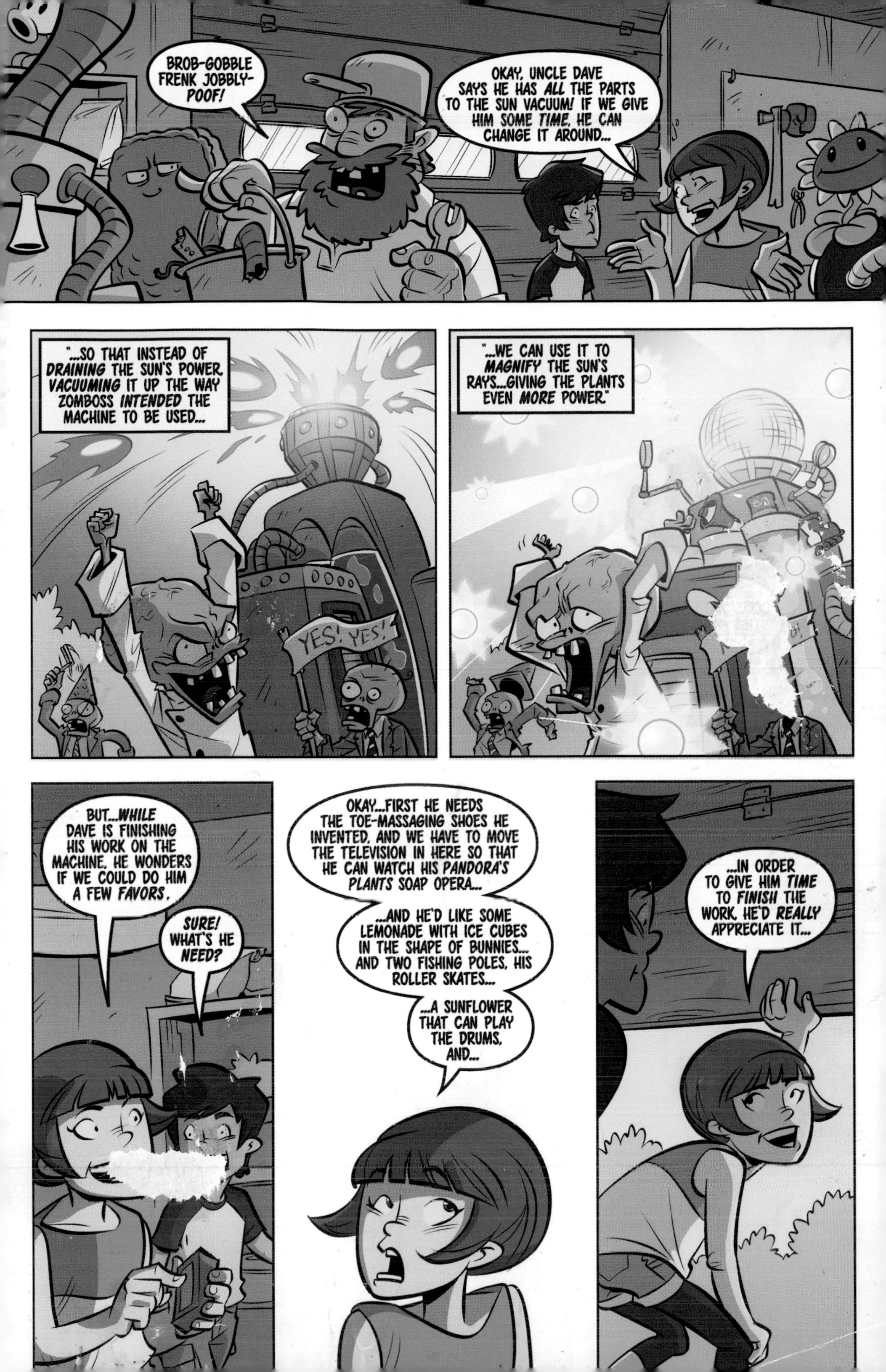
BROB-GOBBLE FRENK JOBBLY-POOF!
OKAY, UNCLE DAVE SAYS HE HAS ALL THE PARTS TO THE SUN VACUUM! IF WE GIVE HIM SOME TIME, HE CAN CHANGE IT AROUND...
"...SO THAT INSTEAD OF DRAINING THE SUN'S POWER, VACUUMING IT UP THE WAY ZOMBOSS INTENDED THE MACHINE TO BE USED...
YES! YES!
"...WE CAN USE IT TO MAGNIFY THE SUN'S RAYS...GIVING THE PLANTS EVEN MORE POWER."
BUT...WHILE DAVE IS FINISHING HIS WORK ON THE MACHINE, HE WONDERS IF WE COULD DO HIM A FEW FAVORS.
SURE! WHAT'S HE NEED?
OKAY...FIRST HE NEEDS THE TOE-MASSAGING SHOES HE INVENTED, AND WE HAVE TO MOVE THE TELEVISION IN HERE SO THAT HE CAN WATCH HIS PANDORA'S PLANTS SOAP OPERA...
...AND HE'D LIKE SOME LEMONADE WITH ICE CUBES IN THE SHAPE OF BUNNIES... AND TWO FISHING POLES, HIS ROLLER SKATES...
...A SUNFLOWER THAT CAN PLAY THE DRUMS, AND...
...IN ORDER TO GIVE HIM TIME TO FINISH THE WORK, HE'D REALLY APPRECIATE IT...

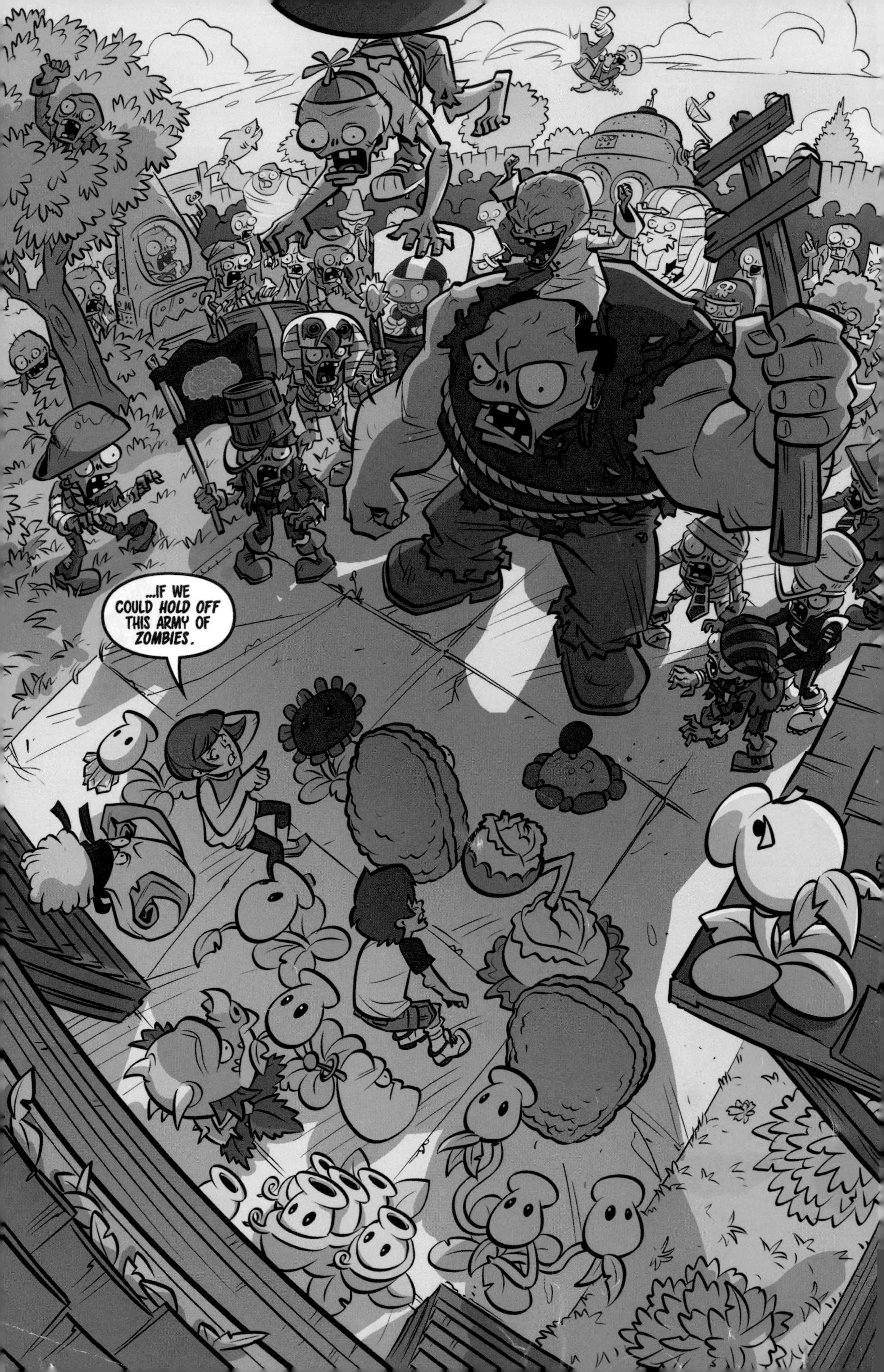
...IF WE COULD HOLD OFF THIS ARMY OF ZOMBIES.

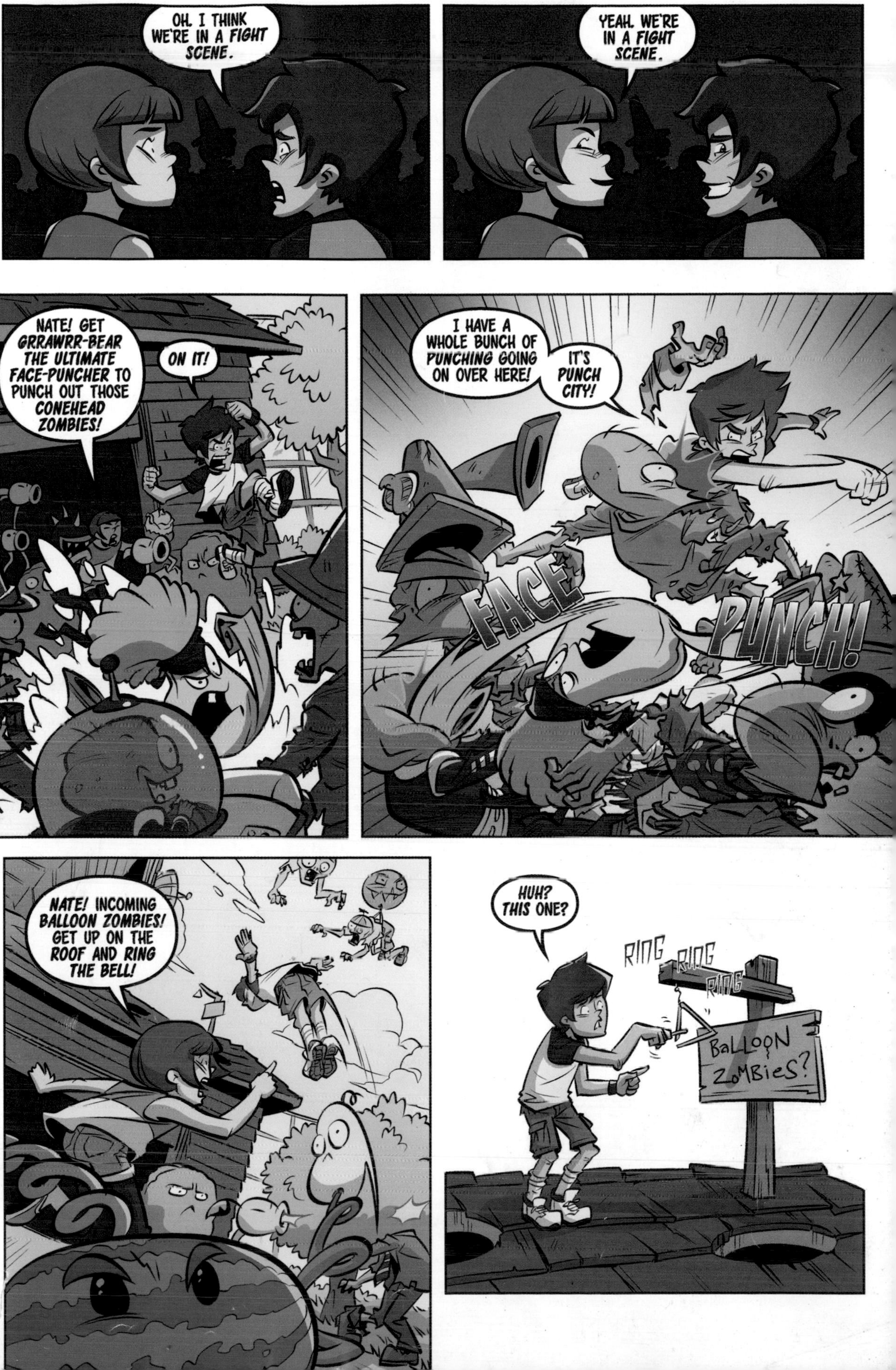
OH. I THINK WE'RE IN A FIGHT SCENE.
YEAH. WE'RE IN A FIGHT SCENE.
NATE! GET GRRAWRR-BEAR THE ULTIMATE FACE-PUNCHER TO PUNCH OUT THOSE CONEHEAD ZOMBIES!
ON IT!
I HAVE A WHOLE BUNCH OF PUNCHING GOING ON OVER HERE!
IT'S PUNCH CITY!
FACE
PUNCH!
NATE! INCOMING BALLOON ZOMBIES! GET UP ON THE ROOF AND RING THE BELL!
HUH? THIS ONE?
RING
RING
RING
BALLOON ZOMBIES?

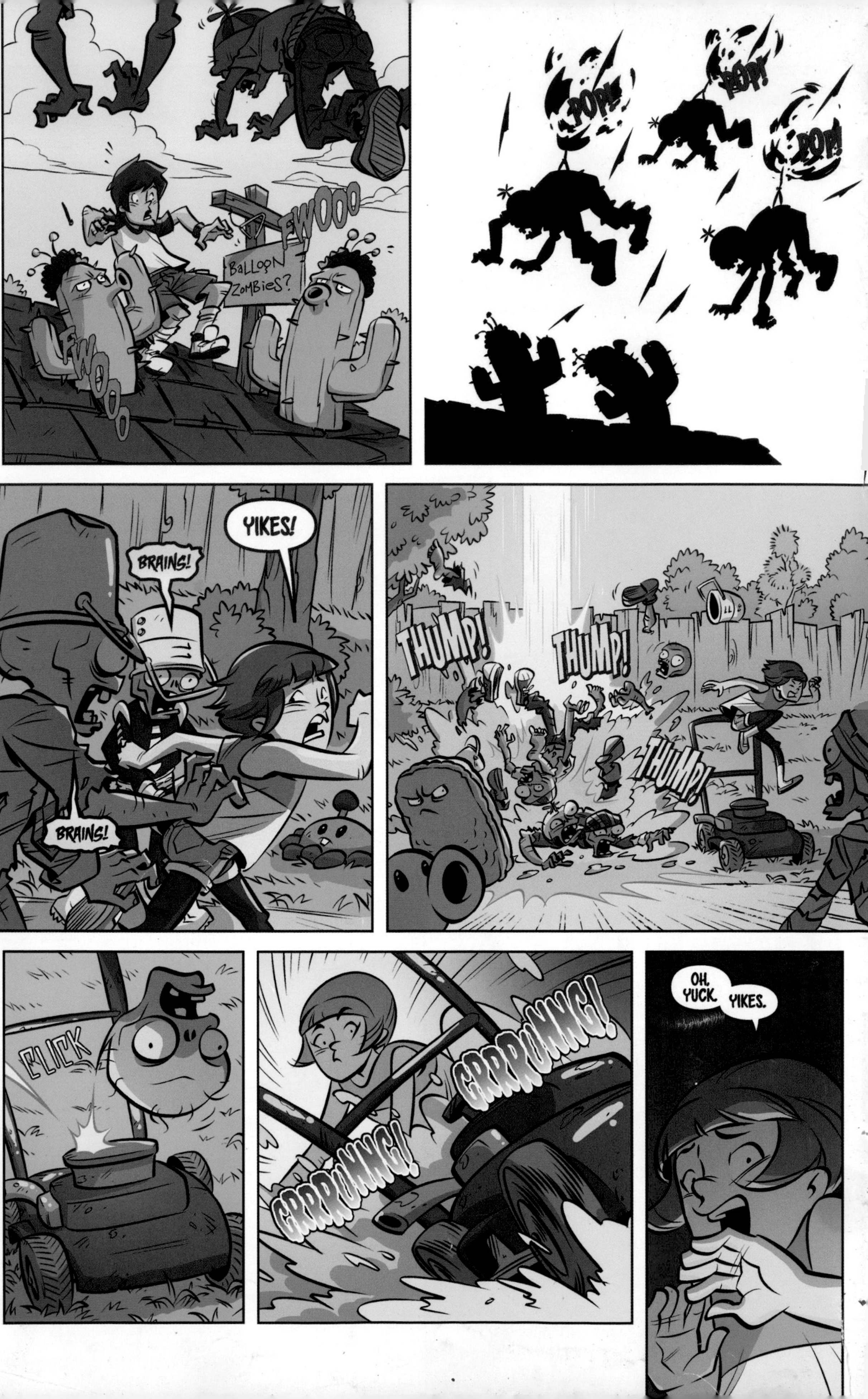

BALLOON ZOMBIES?
FWOOO
FWOOO
POP!
POP!
POP!
BRAINS!
YIKES!
BRAINS!
THUMP!
THUMP!
THUMP!
CLICK
CRRRUNNG!
CRRRUNNG!
OH, YUCK.
YIKES.

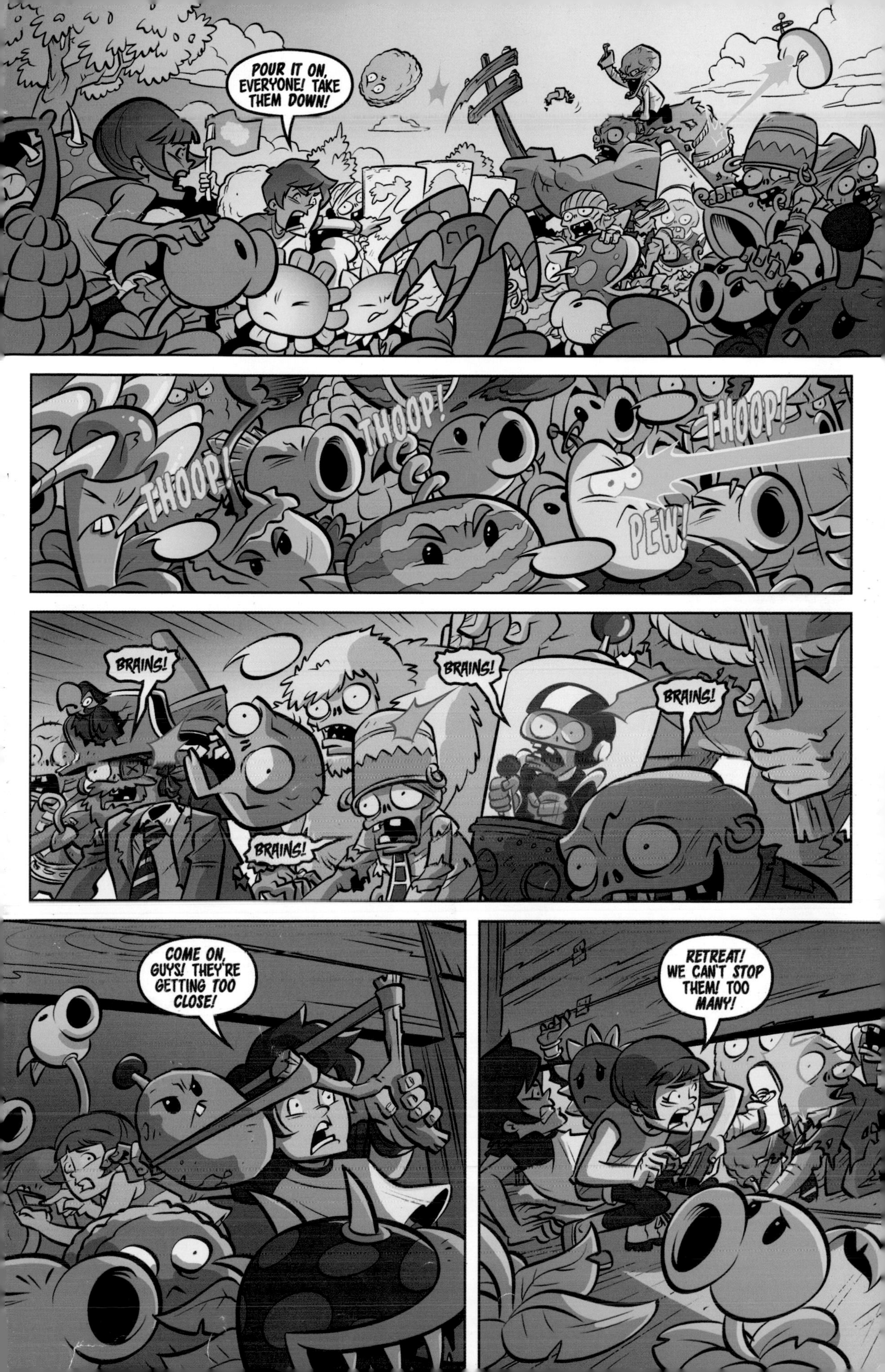
POUR IT ON, EVERYONE! TAKE THEM DOWN!
THOOP!
THOOP!
THOOP!
PEW!
BRAINS!
BRAINS!
BRAINS!
BRAINS!
COME ON, GUYS! THEY'RE GETTING TOO CLOSE!
RETREAT! WE CAN'T STOP THEM! TOO MANY!

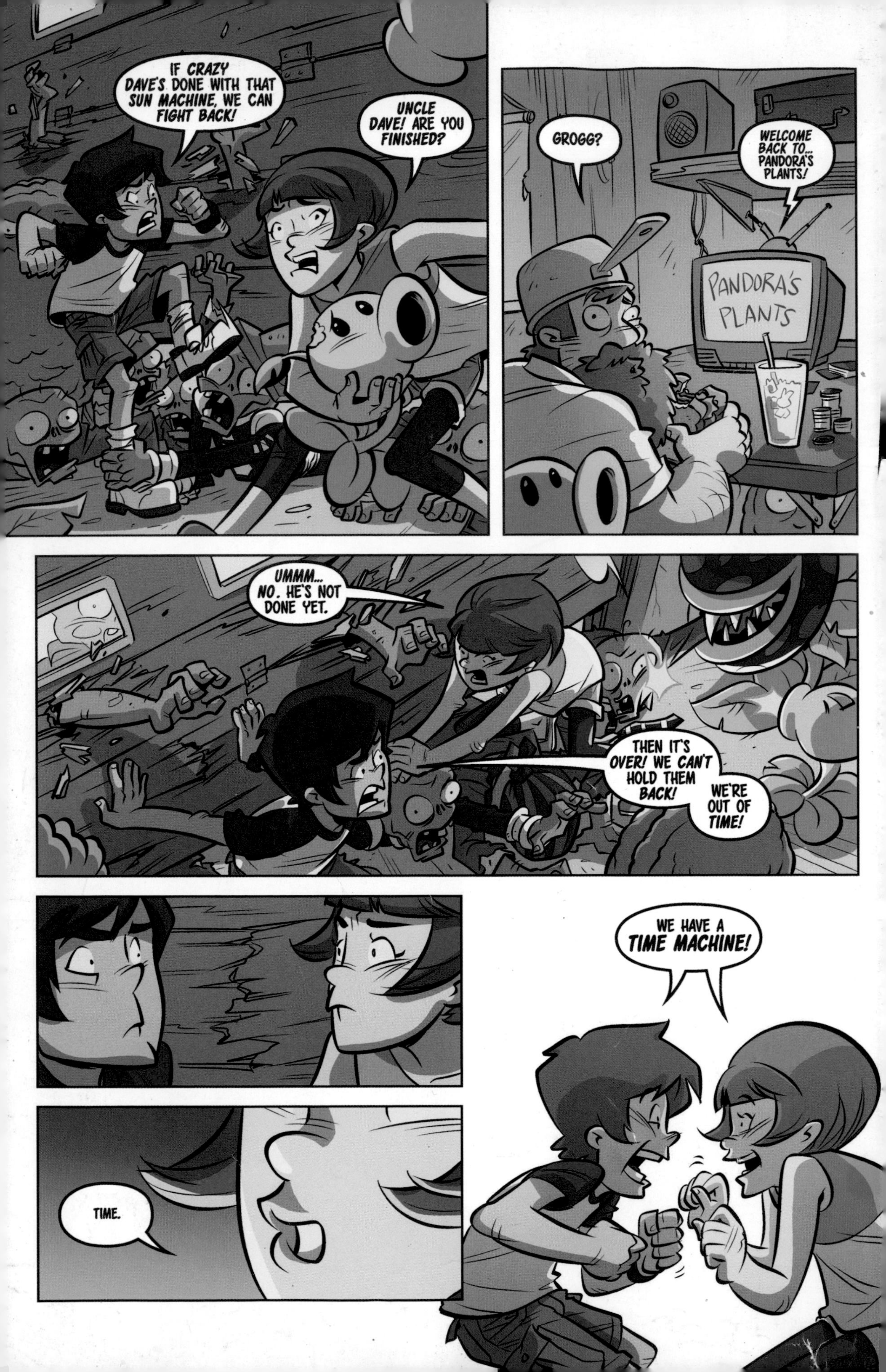
IF CRAZY DAVE'S DONE WITH THAT SUN MACHINE, WE CAN FIGHT BACK!
UNCLE DAVE! ARE YOU FINISHED?
GROGG?
WELCOME BACK TO... PANDORA'S PLANTS!
PANDORA'S PLANTS
UMMM... NO. HE'S NOT DONE YET.
THEN IT'S OVER! WE CAN'T HOLD THEM BACK!
WE'RE OUT OF TIME!
TIME.
WE HAVE A TIME MACHINE!

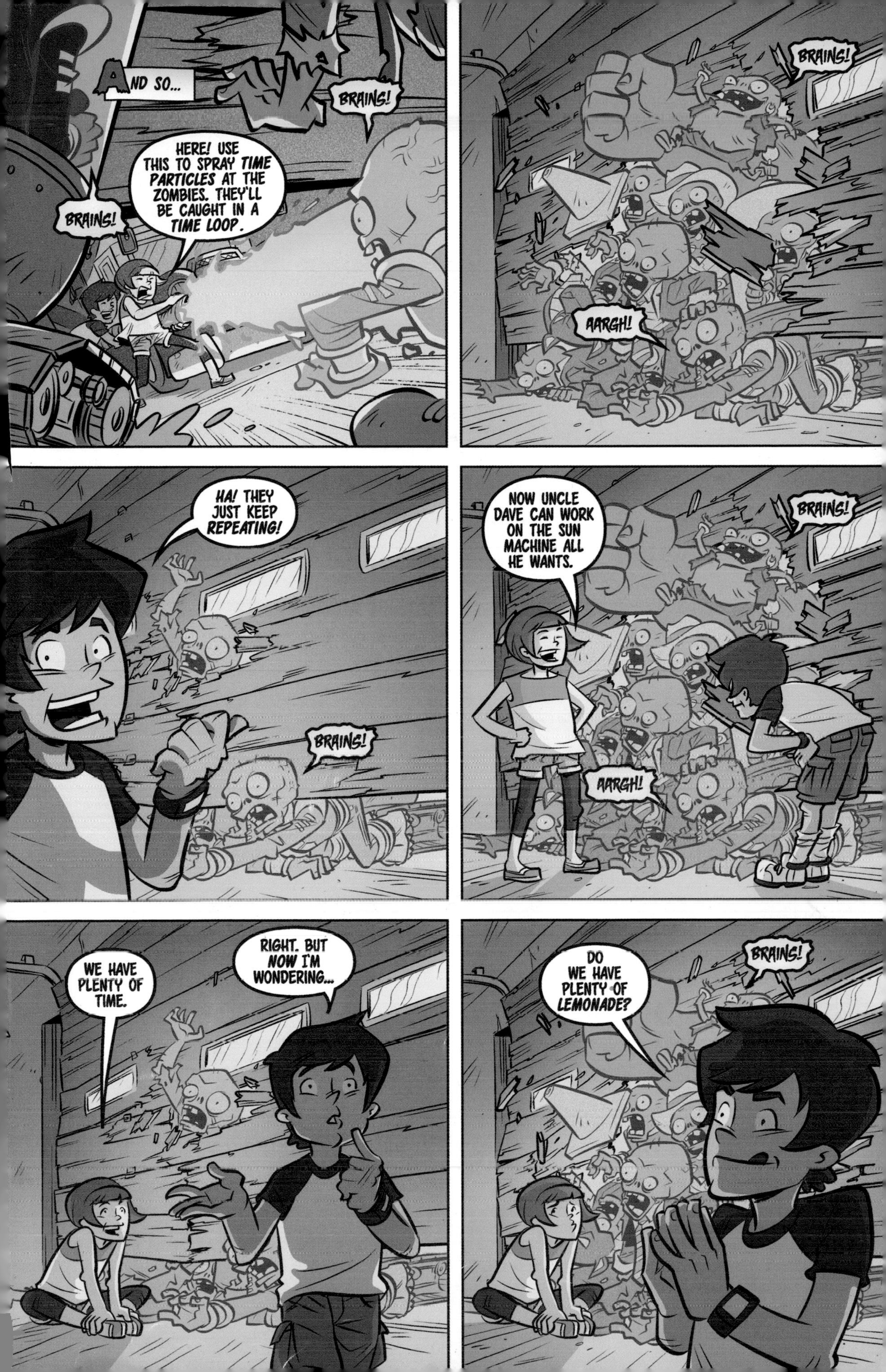
AND SO...
BRAINS!
HERE! USE THIS TO SPRAY TIME PARTICLES AT THE ZOMBIES. THEY'LL BE CAUGHT IN A TIME LOOP.
BRAINS!
BRAINS!
AARGH!
HA! THEY JUST KEEP REPEATING!
BRAINS!
NOW UNCLE DAVE CAN WORK ON THE SUN MACHINE ALL HE WANTS.
BRAINS!
AARGH!
WE HAVE PLENTY OF TIME.
RIGHT. BUT NOW I'M WONDERING...
DO WE HAVE PLENTY OF LEMONADE?
BRAINS!

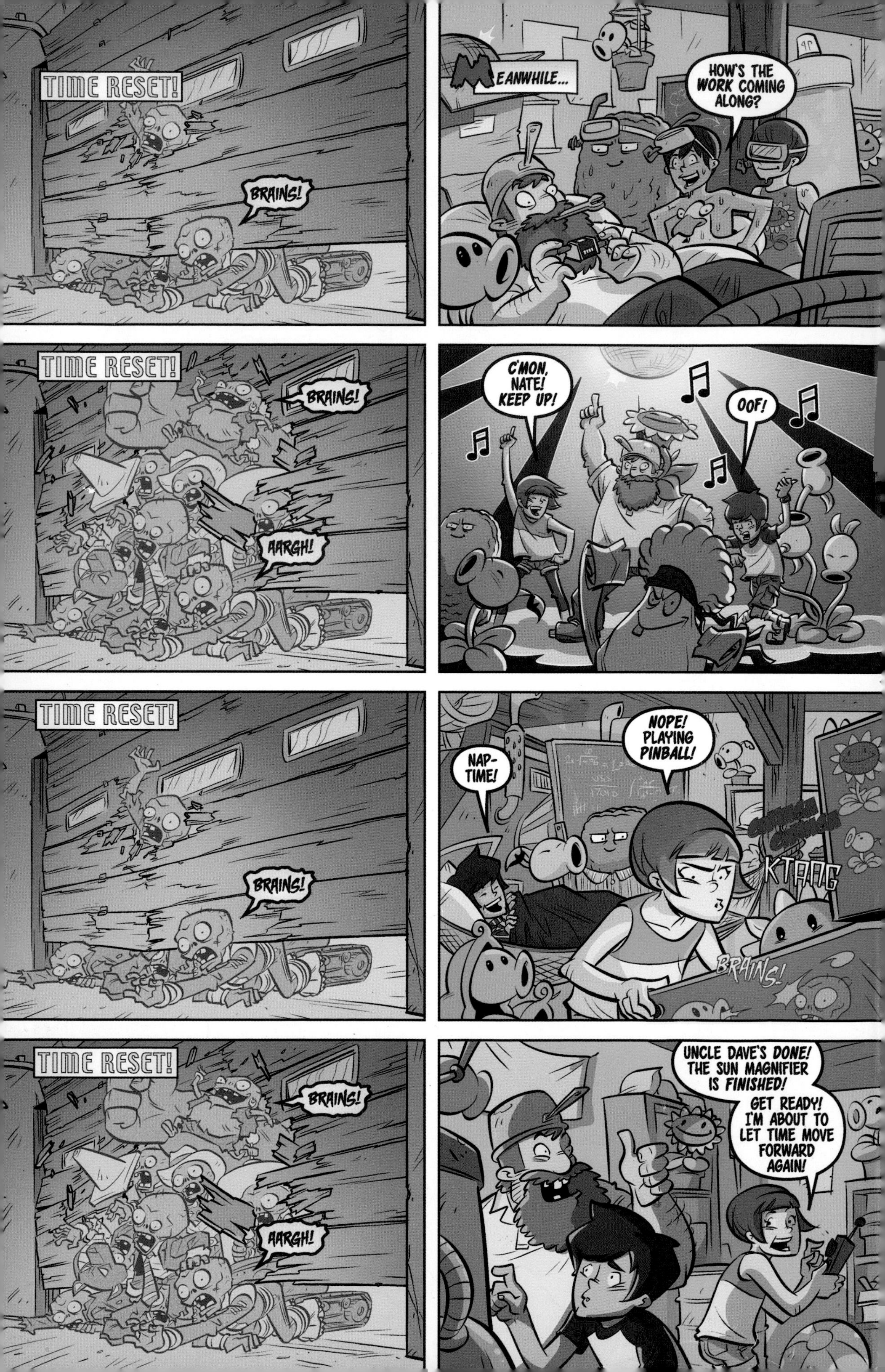

TIME RESET!
BRAINS!
MEANWHILE...
HOW'S THE WORK COMING ALONG?
TIME RESET!
BRAINS!
AARGH!
C'MON, NATE! KEEP UP!
OOF!
TIME RESET!
BRAINS!
NAP-TIME!
NOPE! PLAYING PINBALL!
KTANG
BRAINS!
TIME RESET!
BRAINS!
AARGH!
UNCLE DAVE'S DONE! THE SUN MAGNIFIER IS FINISHED!
GET READY! I'M ABOUT TO LET TIME MOVE FORWARD AGAIN!

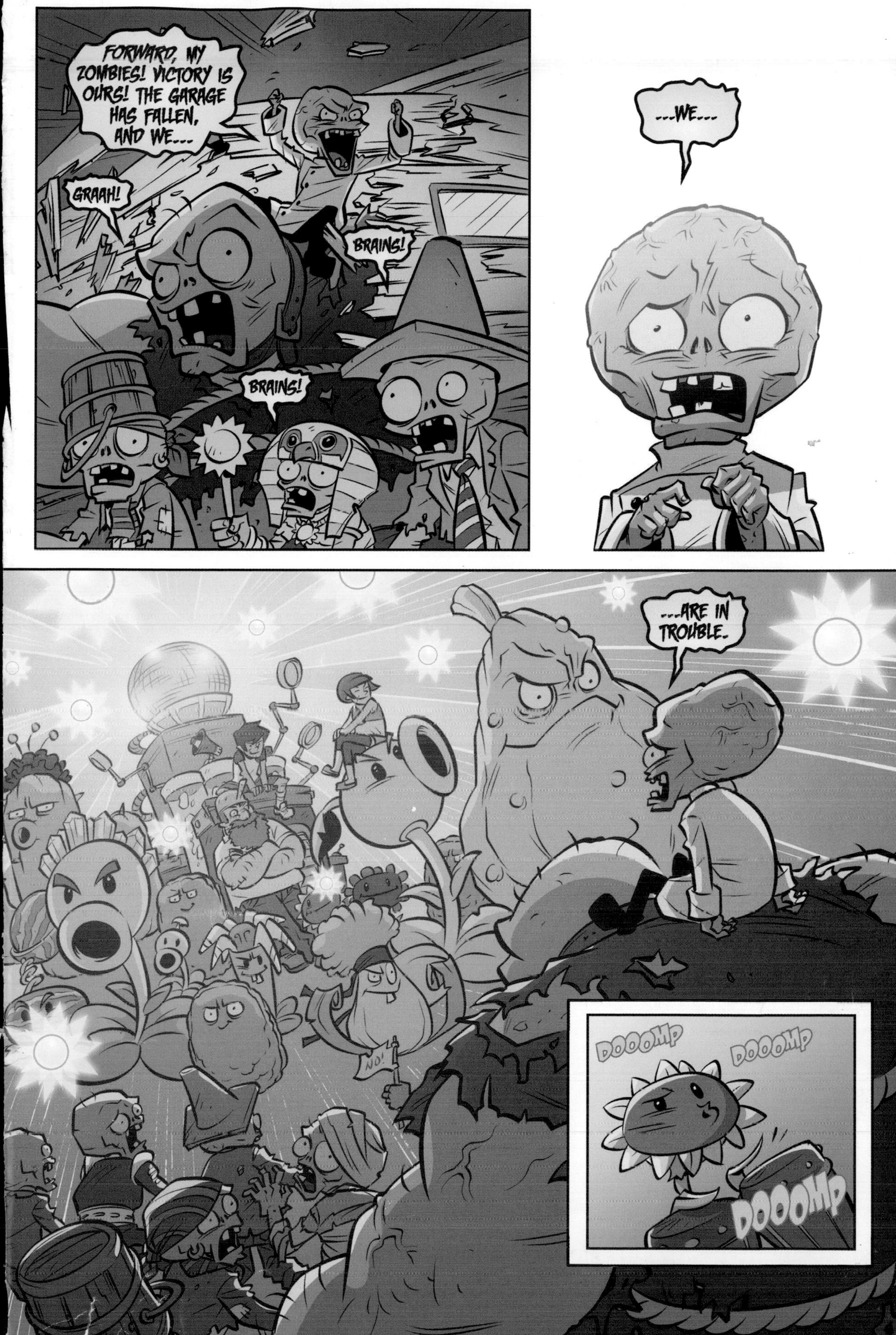
FORWARD, MY ZOMBIES! VICTORY IS OURS! THE GARAGE HAS FALLEN, AND WE...
GRAAH!
BRAINS!
BRAINS!
...WE...
...ARE IN TROUBLE.
NO!
DOOOMP
DOOOMP
DOOOMP

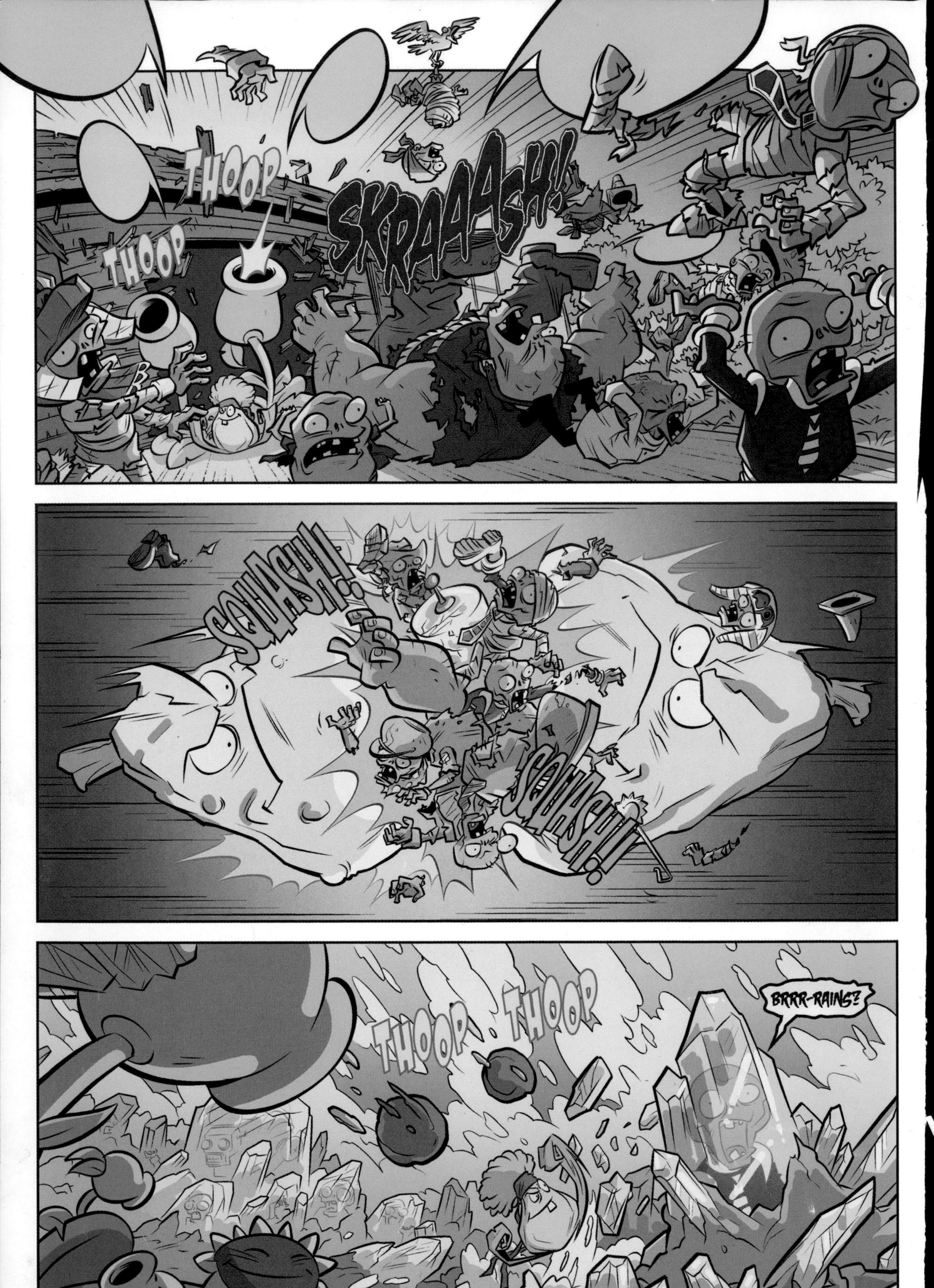
THOOP
THOOP
SKRAAASH!!
SQUASH!!
SQUASH!!
THOOP
THOOP
BRRR-RAINS?

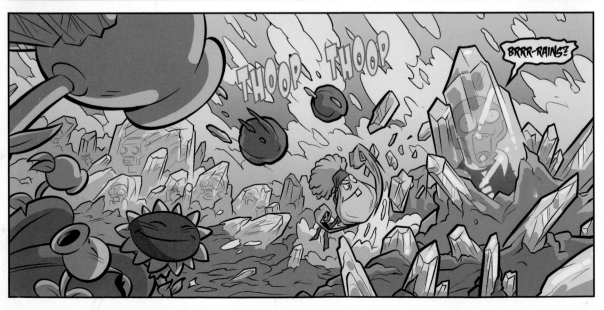

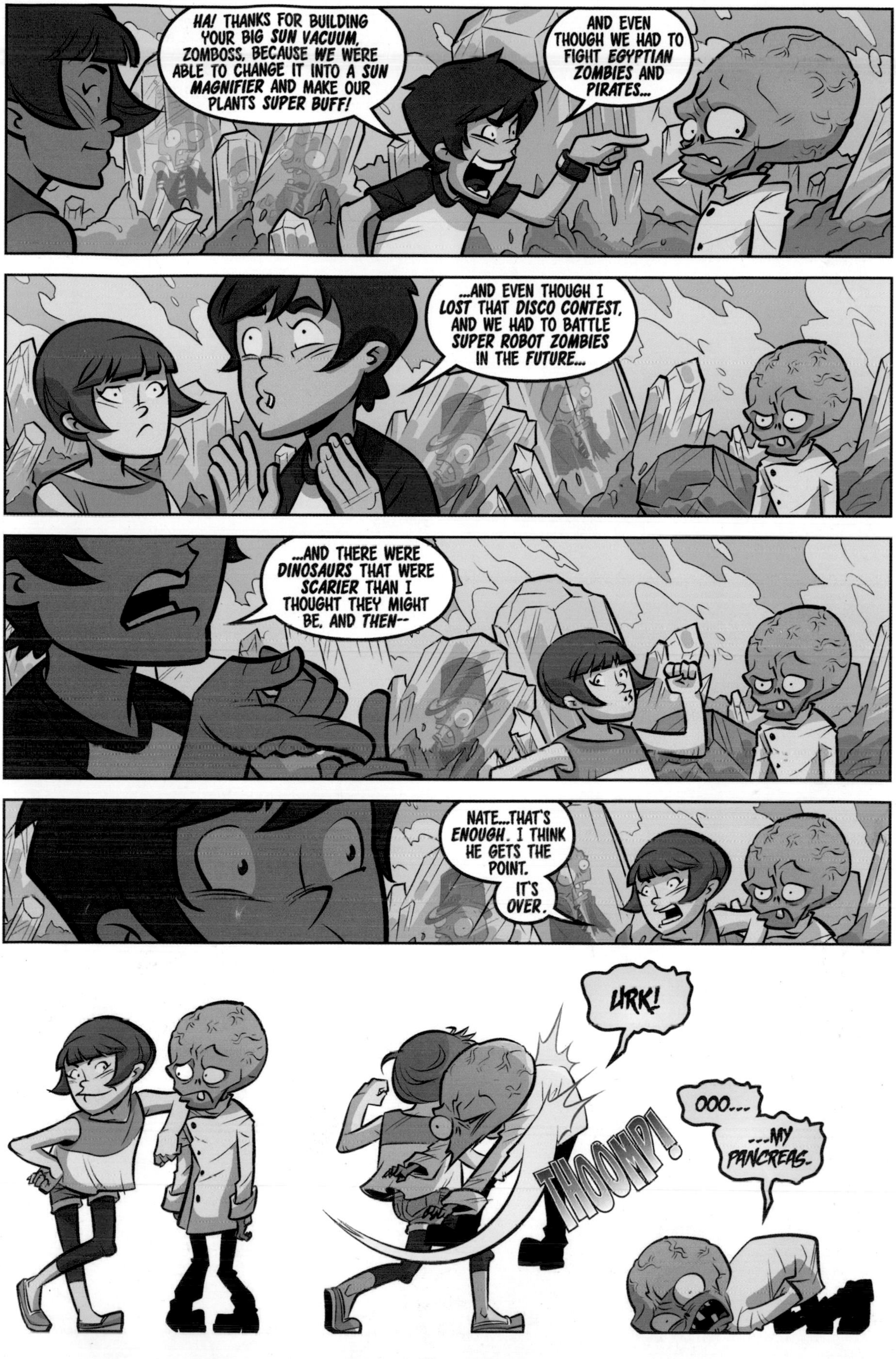
HA! THANKS FOR BUILDING YOUR BIG SUN VACUUM, ZOMBOSS, BECAUSE WE WERE ABLE TO CHANGE IT INTO A SUN MAGNIFIER AND MAKE OUR PLANTS SUPER BUFF!
AND EVEN THOUGH WE HAD TO FIGHT EGYPTIAN ZOMBIES AND PIRATES...
...AND EVEN THOUGH I LOST THAT DISCO CONTEST, AND WE HAD TO BATTLE SUPER ROBOT ZOMBIES IN THE FUTURE...
...AND THERE WERE DINOSAURS THAT WERE SCARIER THAN I THOUGHT THEY MIGHT BE, AND THEN--
NATE...THAT'S ENOUGH. I THINK HE GETS THE POINT.
IT'S OVER.
URK!
THOOMP!
OOO...
...MY PANCREAS.

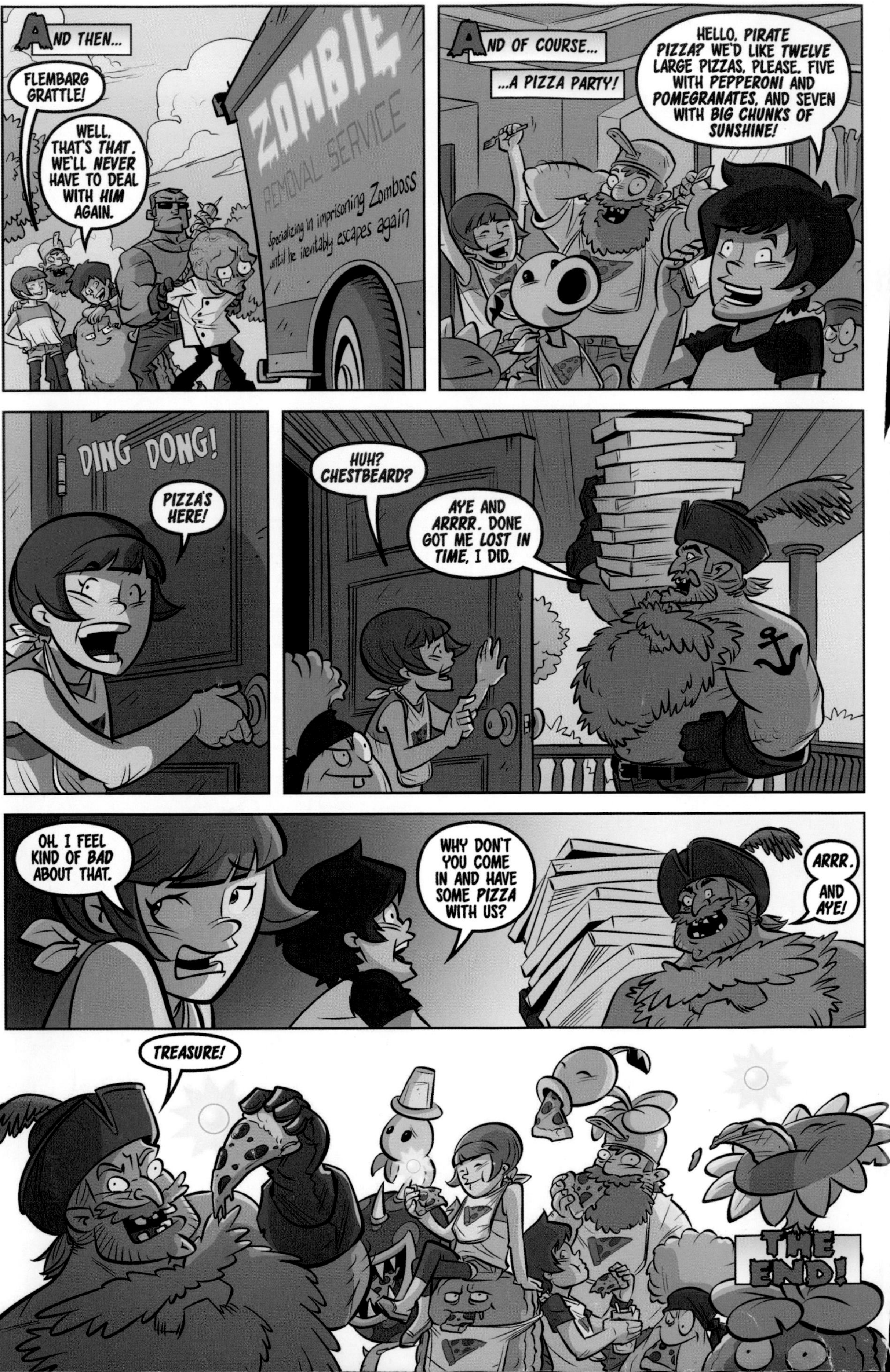
AND THEN...
FLEMBARG GRATTLE!
WELL, THAT'S THAT. WE'LL NEVER HAVE TO DEAL WITH HIM AGAIN.
ZOMBIE REMOVAL SERVICE
Specializing in imprisoning Zomboss until he inevitably escapes again
AND OF COURSE...
...A PIZZA PARTY!
HELLO, PIRATE PIZZA? WE'D LIKE TWELVE LARGE PIZZAS, PLEASE. FIVE WITH PEPPERONI AND POMEGRANATES, AND SEVEN WITH BIG CHUNKS OF SUNSHINE!
DING DONG!
PIZZA'S HERE!
HUH? CHESTBEARD?
AYE AND ARRRR. DONE GOT ME LOST IN TIME, I DID.
OH, I FEEL KIND OF BAD ABOUT THAT.
WHY DON'T YOU COME IN AND HAVE SOME PIZZA WITH US?
ARRR.
AND AYE!
TREASURE!
THE END!